國家圖書館出版品預行編目資料

NEW TOEIC新多益聽力測驗大滿貫關鍵攻略：

擬真試題+超詳解析 / 張文娟著. -- 初版.

-- 新北市：雅典文化，民111. 08

面；　公分. --（英語工具書；17）

ISBN 978-626-95952-5-9（平裝）

1. CTS: 多益測驗

805. 1895　　　　　　　　　　111007986

英語工具書系列 **17**

NEW TOEIC新多益聽力測驗大滿貫關鍵攻略：擬真試題+超詳解析

著／張文娟

責任編輯／張文娟

內文排版／王國卿

封面設計／林鈺恆

法律顧問：方圓法律事務所／涂成樞律師

總經銷：永續圖書有限公司

永續圖書線上購物網
www.foreverbooks.com.tw

掃描填回函
好書隨時抽

出版日／2022年08月

雅典文化

出版社　22103　新北市汐止區大同路三段194號9樓之1

TEL　（02）8647-3663

FAX　（02）8647-3660

NEW TOEIC

新多益

聽力測驗

大滿貫關鍵攻略：
擬真試題＋超詳解析

● 前言

　　首先請你於心中想像自己戰勝英語的成功姿態，想著你帶著一張新多益金色高分證書，充滿自信心，順利通過英語面試，進入心中理想的企業或大學，並且在工作一開始就表現出傑出英語能力，讓主管或教授對你刮目相看，同事或同學們紛紛來向你請教英文問題，是的，這一切你一定做得到，因為此時你手中捧的這本書，就是戰勝新多益的利器，只要你願意跟著此書，展開學習英語之旅，就能循序漸進達到最終目的地。

　　想要培養英文能力，在平時不妨將英語當成發展興趣的工具，例如聽英語流行歌曲，這樣子學習到的字彙才會更有意義，也能記得更牢一些，但是現在正在讀此書的你，可能有非常迫切的職場需要，必須要於短時間內獲得新多益的一定高分，那麼，一本能符合應考需求的專書就格外重要了。本書就是針對這個目的而寫，希望在新多益聽力上能提供讀者一臂之力，使考生能夠在有限的準備時間內，熟練破解新多益多變的考題，輕鬆過關斬將，獲得金色證書或理想中的分數。

設定學習目標

　　為了激勵學習英語的動力，設定合適的短中長期的目標是很重要的，這樣才比較不會於學習途中彈性疲乏，導致無法繼續下去，也別忘了要當自己最好的啦啦隊，隨時鼓勵自己，最好於達成一個目標後適時犒賞自己，例如短期目標：看完本書某章節，就請自己上高檔餐廳；中期目標：完成模擬試題，就去三天兩夜的旅遊；至於獲得金色證書這樣的長期目標，就可以出國旅遊等等。

專注力與時間管理

　　學習英語常常會遇到進步緩慢，停滯不前的一段高原期，研讀本書可以幫助你縮短高原期，找出應對策略，改進學習方法，善巧克服困難，突破學習英語的關卡。在新多益測驗中，持久的專注力非常重要，只有專心一致，才能按著本書中的要訣，破解各題型。

　　因為新多益聽力測驗是用正常英語速度，因此有不少人感覺跟不上，很多人抱怨在考試時間內無法做完題目，閱讀題目還可再讀一次，而聽力題只有播放一次，所以練習加快速度非常重要，多做模擬考題，對於加快答題速度很有助益，而這樣加快速度的自我訓練，在實際工作上的英語應用也非常重要。

　　時間管理在學習英語非常重要，一般而言，每天花一點時間學英語，比間隔一大段日子，然後學一整天來得有效，當然這也需要依個人的學習狀況與真實生活來調整，總之，想要成就任何事，時間管理都是關鍵，尤其在這個瞬息萬變的時代裡，更是如此。

考場與職場英語都大收穫

　　有人說新多益 2018 年改制後的聽力分數比閱讀分數容易提升，因為閱讀的複雜性導致難度增加不少，如果是這樣的話，更希望各位讀者都能花心思來研讀本書，按部就班準備新多益測驗，尤其是本書中巧心安排的精華整理，能有助於有效率獲得新多益的聽力高分，連帶使在職場的英語實用能力大幅進步，這樣子才能一箭雙鵰，獲得新多益與真實職場上的英語高能力。根據通過新多益測驗者的經驗談，在準備與考過新多益測驗之後，很多都發現自己在工作時更能應用職場英語了。

前言 005

Chapter

1 NEW TOEIC 簡介 010

Chapter

2 新制 NEW TOEIC 022

Chapter

3 聽英語的要點 028

一、連音

二、語調

三、聽音辨義

四、各國口音

五、英語生活化口語用法

六、用情境來聯想單字

Chapter

4 破解聽力各 Parts 056

Part 1

    1. 注意重點

    2. 出題類型

Part 2

    1. 注意重點

    2. 出題類型

    3. 應對策略

Part 3

    1. 注意重點

    2. 出題類型

    3. 常見場景

Part 4

    1. 注意重點

    2. 出題類型

    3. 常見場景

Chapter

5 聽力模擬試題 324

後記

New TOEIC

New TOEIC

New TOEIC

1

NEW TOEIC 簡介

● 本章以 Q&A（問答方式）來解說新多益測驗：

Q 1 ：什麼是新多益英語測驗（TOEIC）？

A ：

　　新多益英語測驗（TOEIC）全名為 Test of English for International Communication，是美國教育測驗服務社（Educational Testing Service, ETS）針對母語非英語人士所研發的英語能力測驗，全球每年有超過700萬人次報考。

　　新多益系列測驗（The TOEICProgram）目前可於全球160個國家施測，至少為1萬4千個以上的企業客戶、教育單位及政府機構所採用。成績不僅具備信度與效度，也具有國際流通度，足以體現考生在實際溝通情境中的英語文能力。

　　TOEICListening and Reading Test本身並沒有所謂的「通過」或「不通過」，而是客觀地將受測者的能力以聽力5～495分、閱讀5～495分、總分10～990分的指標呈現，受測者也可以自評現在的英語能力，進而設定學習的目標分數。

Q 2：TOEIC 多益的測驗用途為何？

A：

在真實的職場與校園環境中，當需要以英語溝通時，透過新多益系列測驗，成績使用單位能夠進一步掌握職員與學習者的能力現況。

也因為新多益系列測驗之國際流通度廣闊，眾多國內外企業、學校，皆採用新多益系列測驗作為評核人才英語程度之標準。

(一)求學加分條件

★ 升學加分證照

109 學年度大學個人申請簡章中，超過 1,000 個招生校系將「英文能力證明」列為審查資料或加分條件，善用新多益系列測驗成績，點亮大學甄選、四技二專甄選備審資料。

★ 登錄學習歷程

自 108 學年度起，教育部高中生學習歷程資料庫正式全面上線，新多益系列測驗成績可登錄「高中數位學習歷程檔案資料庫」，作為學生的多元表現認證之一，且登錄數量無上限。

★ 大學英文免修門檻、英語班級程度分班

國內超過百所大學採用新多益系列測驗作為英文課程免修門檻;學校亦可用新多益系列測驗成績作為大一英語分班標準。

(二)求職加分條件

★ 求職履歷加分,提升職場競爭力

據調查,400 家年營收超過 1 億元新台幣的企業中,超過六成(62.1%)企業招募新人會參考英語成績。且要求新進員工平均新多益成績為 582 分。想展現求職優勢者,可運用新多益成績點亮履歷,在眾多競爭者中脫穎而出。

★ 就業升遷標準、企業人才管理工具

2012 至 2018 年,使用新多益系列測驗的企業逐漸增加,2018 年有 36%的企業選擇新多益系列測驗掌握員工實際的英語程度,作為企業員工招募、升遷及外派標準、企業人才管理工具。

★ 教學管理、人才篩選標準

★ 英語文教學管理指標

英語教學機構可善用新多益系列測驗落實英語能力管理,作為英語課程前測、教學成果評量,以及英語培訓績效檢驗標準。

★ 國際志工選拔評量標準

舉凡國際會議、體育賽事等活動，採用新多益系列測驗成績作為選拔國際志工的標準。運用新多益成績突顯英語優勢，爭取參與國際活動的機會。

Q 3：TOEIC 多益的研發製作單位為何？

ETS®是目前全球規模最大的一所非營利教育測驗及評量單位，在全球180多個國家／地區提供服務，每年開發、管理和評分超過5000萬次考試。

ETS®專精教學評量及測驗心理學、教育政策之研究，在教學研究領域上居於領導地位，擁有教育專家、語言學家、統計學家、心理學家等成員約3,200名。其研發的測驗及語言學習產品包括：TOEFL iBT® Test、TOEFL ITP® Tests、TOEFL Junior® Standard Tests、TOEFL® Primary™ Tests、TOEIC® Tests、TOEIC Bridge® Tests、SAT®、GRE® 測驗等，以及CRITERION®。

Q 4：TOEIC 多益的測驗內容為何？

A：

本測驗針對母語非英語人士所設計，測驗題型反映全球現有日常生活中，社交及職場之英語使用情況。測驗題型多元化，涵蓋多種場合、地點與狀況。能檢驗出考生目前或未來在真實情境中所需的國際溝通力。

TOEIC® Listening and Reading Test 共 200 題，皆為單選題，分為聽力及閱讀兩大部分，測驗時間約 2 小時 30 分鐘（含基本資料及問卷填寫）。

TOEIC Listening and Reading Test			
《聽力測驗》	**Part1** 照片描述	**Part2** 應答問題	**Part3** 簡短對話	**Part4** 簡短獨白
《閱讀測驗》	**Part5** 句子填空	**Part6** 段落填空	**Part7** 閱讀測驗	

聽力測驗

　　包含 4 大題，共 100 個單選題，測驗時間約為 45 分鐘，內容包含四種口音，以及多種題型如應答問題、簡短對話等。

大題	題型	題數
1	照片描述	6題
2	應答問題	25題
3	簡短對話3	9題(3x13)
4	簡短獨白	30題(3x10)

閱讀測驗

　　包含 3 大題，共 100 個單選題，測驗時間為 75 分鐘。內容包含網頁、通訊軟體、網站等閱讀題材，並依個人能力調配閱讀及答題速度。

大題	題型	題數
5	句子填空	30題
6	段落填空	16題(4x4)
7	單篇閱讀	29題
	多篇閱讀	25題

Q 5 ： TOEIC 多益的測驗情境有哪些？

A ：

企業發展	研究、產品研發
外食	商務／非正式午餐、宴會、招待會、餐廳訂位
娛樂	電影、劇場、音樂、藝術、展覽、博物館、媒體
金融／預算	銀行業務、投資、稅務、會計、帳單
一般商務	契約、談判、併購、行銷、銷售、保證、商業企劃、會議、勞動關係
保健	醫療保險、看醫生、牙醫、診所、醫院
房屋／公司地產	建築、規格、購買租賃、電力瓦斯服務
製造業	工廠管理、生產線、品管
辦公室	董事會、委員會、信件、備忘錄、電話、傳真、電子郵件、辦公室器材與家俱、公室流程
人事	招考、雇用、退休、薪資、升遷、應徵與廣告、津貼、獎勵
採購	購物、訂購物資、送貨、發票
技術層面	電子、科技、電腦、實驗室與相關器材、技術規格
旅遊	火車、飛機、計程車、巴士、船隻、渡輪、票務、時刻表、車站、機場廣播、租車、飯店、預定、脫班與取消

Q 6 ：TOEIC 多益的測驗如何計分？

A ：

　　考生用鉛筆在答案卡上作答。測驗分數取決於由答對題數決定，再將每一大類（聽力類、閱讀類）答對題數轉換成分數，範圍在5到495分之間。兩大類加起來即為總分，範圍在10到990分之間，答錯不倒扣。

證書說明

　　TOEIC證書中列出聽力與閱讀的分項分數及總分，依考生成績分為五種顏色，是職場競爭力的最佳證明，測驗日起兩年內都可申請。

證書分類

- 金色 860～990 分
- 藍色 730～855 分
- 綠色 470～725 分
- 棕色 220～465 分
- 橘色 10～215 分

Q 7 ：TOEIC 多益成績如何反映英語能力？

A ：

多益成績與英語能力對照表

TOEIC®	語言能力	證照顏色
905~990	英語能力十分近似於英語母語人士，能夠流暢有條理表達意見、參與談話，主持英文會議、調和衝突並做出結論，語言使用上即使有瑕疵，亦不會造成理解上的困擾。	金色(860~990)
785~900	可有效地運用英文滿足社交及工作上所需，措辭相當、表達流暢；但在某些情形下，如：面臨緊張壓力、討論話題過於冷僻艱澀時，仍會顯現出語言能力不足的情況。	金色(860~990) 藍色(730~855)
605~780	可以英語進行一般社交場會的談話，能夠應付例行性的業務需求、參加英文會議、聽取大部分要點；但無法流利的以英語發表意見、作辯論，使用的詞彙、句型也以一般常見為主。	藍色(730~855) 綠色(470~725)
405~600	英文文字溝通能力尚可，會話方面稍嫌詞彙不足、語句簡單，但已能掌握少量相關語言，可以從事英語相關程度較低的工作。	綠色(470~725) 棕色(220~465)
255~400	語言能力僅僅侷限在簡單的一般日常生活對話，同時無法做連續性交談，亦無法用英文工作。	棕色(220~465) 橘色(10~215)
10~250	只能以背誦的句子進行問答而不能自行造句，尚無法將英文當作溝通工具來使用。	橘色(10~215)

Q 8：台灣各行各業對多益分數的要求為何？

A：

(一) TOEIC 多益測驗約 100-215 分＝初級

有基礎英語能力，能理解和使用淺易日常用語，英語能力相當於國中畢業者。一般行政助理、維修技術人員、百貨業、餐飲業、旅館業或觀光景點服務人員、計程車駕駛等。

(二) TOEIC 多益測驗約 220-465 分＝中級

具有使用簡單英語進行日常生活溝通的能力，英語能力相當於高中職畢業者。一般地勤行政、業務、技術、銷售人員、護理人員、旅館、飯店接待人員、總機人員、警政人員、旅遊從業人員等。

(三) TOEIC 多益測驗約 470-725 分＝中高級

英語能力相當於大學非英語主修系所畢業者。商務、企劃人員、祕書、工程師、研究助理、空服人員、航空機師、航管人員、海關人員、導遊、外事警政人員、新聞從業人員、資訊管理人員等。

(四) TOEIC 多益測驗約 730-855 分＝高級

　　英語能力相當於國內大學英語主修系所或曾赴英語系國家大學或研究所進修並取得學位者。高級商務人員、協商談判人員、英語教學人員、研究人員、翻譯人員、外交人員、國際新聞從業人員等。

(五) TOEIC 多益測驗約 860-990 分＝優級

　　英語能力接近受過高等教育之母語人士，各種場合均能使用適當策略作最有效的溝通。專業翻譯人員、國際新聞特派人員、外交官員、協商談判主談人員等。

　　以上資料來源為http://www.toeic.com.tw/

New TOEIC
New TOEIC
New TOEIC

2

新制 NEW TOEIC

本章以 Q&A（問答方式）來解說改版後的新多益：

Q 1 ： 2018 年 3 月為什麼會推出改版的新多益？

A ：

　　為確保測驗符合考生及成績使用單位之需求，ETS定期重新檢視所有試題內容。TOEIC®Listening and Reading Test題型更新，反映了全球現有日常生活中社交及職場之英語使用情況。作為一個評量日常生活或職場情境之英語測驗，依然維持相同的公平性、效度以及信度。本次測驗更新，題型雖有所改變，但測驗的難易度、測驗時間或測驗分數所代表的意義將不會有所變動。

　　由於英語的使用及溝通方法不斷改變，為了確保TO-EIC® Listening and Reading Test能夠反映出時下英語使用的狀況，ETS®更新了部分題型，與時俱進地加入過去十年間經常使用的溝通用語，包括文字簡訊、即時通訊及多人對話等等。 台灣地區自2018年3月份公開測驗開始實施。

Q 2 ： 2018 改版後的新多益測驗題型變更為何？

A ：

　　2018 新制新多益考題數量 200題&考試時間不變 120分鐘。

題型 5 大改變：

1. 聽力照片＆應答題大幅減少
2. 聽力對話從 2 人，增加為 3 人對話
3. 聽力對話 & 獨白加入圖表
4. 閱讀的短文填空仿照托福，加入全新句子插入題
5. 閱讀測驗新增多篇閱讀（3 篇以上文章）

《重點整理》2018 新新多益題型變更

題型		改制前	2018 改制後	差別
聽力測驗：45分鐘				
Part 1	照片題	10 題	6 題	題數減少
Part 2	應答題	30 題	25 題	題數減少
Part 3	短對話	3 題 (共 10 組)	3 題 (共 13 組)	題數增加 加入 3 人對話 加入圖表
Part 4	短獨白	3 題 (共 10 組)	3 題 (共 10 組)	加入圖表
閱讀測驗：75分鐘				
Part 5	單句填空	40 題	30 題	題數大幅減少
Part 6	短文填空	12 題 (共 3 篇)	16 題 (共 4 篇)	題數增加 新增「插入句子題」
Part 7	閱讀測驗	單篇閱讀 共 28 篇 雙篇閱讀 共 20 篇	單篇閱讀 共 29 篇 多篇閱讀 共 25 篇	題數增加 題數增加 增加多篇閱讀

Q 3 ： 2018 改版後的新多益測驗是不是變得比較難？

A ：

2018 新制新多益測驗除了部分題型減少題數，聽力 & 閱讀的部分也分別融入新題型，但考試時間不變，所以難度會提升很多。

以往比較好拿分的題型大幅減少題數，出題方式更靈活、貼近生活，考試需要有良好的英文聽力、閱讀，以及聽讀的整合能力，所以你不但要提升自己的英文能力，閱讀、思考的速度，還有答題速度也要加快很多。新多益成績雖然沒有有效時限，但是現在企業和學校大多要求兩年內的新多益證書，有的甚至更要求要一年內的，關於有效時間的問題，請先詢問一下你的公司或學校。

Q 4 ： 2018 改版後的新多益測驗聽力考題哪裡改變？

A ：

1. 減少簡單、好拿分的「照片題」與「回答問題」題數
2. 「簡短對話」&「簡短獨白」新增圖表：學生要有一心兩用的能力，要邊聽邊看，整合聽與讀，從圖表找出對應的價格、時間等資訊。
3. 「簡短對話」的人數從 2 人增加為 3 人對話，以符合實際的職場狀況。
4. 考題內容「口語化」：加入道地的英文說法。

Q **5** : 2018 改版後的新新多益測驗聽力考題如何準備？

A :

1. 平時要多訓練整合聽讀，注意有數據的圖表，例如英語新聞報導，就會時常出現各種圖表資訊，只要多練習就能跟上速度，聽與讀同時進行，訓練出整合資訊的能力。

2. 多加留意通訊軟體或社群媒體常用的英語用法，如果有使用網路視訊通話，請多留意英語對話與線上交談的用法。

以上資料來源為http://www.toeic.com.tw/

New TOEIC

New TOEIC

New TOEIC

3

聽英語的要點

英語是拼音語言，因此要多用聽的方式來學習，平時訓練聽力的方式有跟讀、覆誦、聽寫等等，多聆聽多模仿，朗朗上口，非常有助於學習。

　　聽英語的時候要留意以下要點：

●一、連音

　　英語中有許多連音的例子，就像我們常說「就〞這樣〞子」，講快了變成了「就〞醬〞子」，英語口語中常常會出現連音，而且是有規則可循的，如果說英語時能夠將連音學得像，能夠讓英語聽起來更道地，更像英語母語者，不過在正式場合，還是要注意是否適用某些連音，尤其在寫作時還是要使用正確寫法，不要將連音拼寫出來。

◆ 英語的連音規則主要有以下幾個規則：

1. 子音」連「母音」

2.「子音」連「同樣的子音」

3.「母音」連「母音」

4. t & d 省音

5. h 省音

列舉：

1. 「子音」連「母音」

第一個字的字尾是子音，第二個字的字首是母音時，連在一起發音。

- let it → letit
  讓它

- want it → wantit
  想要它

- get out → getout
  從何地出來

- a lot of → a lotof
  很多

- Thank you → Thankyou
  謝謝你

- wish you → wi shou
  祝福你

- bless you → ble shou
  賜福於你

- look at → lookat
  看見

- This is → Thiziz
  這是

● **come on** → **comon**
別這樣

● **watch out** → **watchout**
小心

● **give up** → **givup**
放棄

● **stop it** → **stopit**
停止

● **make it** → **makit**
成功

● **name it** → **namit**
命名

2.「子音」連「同樣的子音」

(1)當第一個字的字尾和第二個字的字首發音相同時，同一個音只要發一次。

● **black coffee** → **bla coffee**
黑咖啡

● **tough fight** → **tou fight**
艱辛的奮鬥

● **his student** → **hi student**
他的學生

 track 002

- **fat teacher → fa teacher**
  胖老師

(2) 當第一個字的字尾是t，第二個字的字首是d時，因為t和d的發音位置相同（只差在有聲和無聲的區別），因此第一個字字尾的t不發音。

- **what do → wha do**
  做什麼

- **white dog →whi dog**
  白色的狗

3. 「母音」連「母音」

　　前一個單字的字首和下一個單字的字尾都是母音的話，也可以做連音，但是中間要給他一個滑音，例如：

(1)

[w]滑音

　　當單字最後一個音是母音 [u] 或 [aʊ] 或 [oʊ]（都有 [u] 或 [ʊ] 結尾）時，要把 [w] 作為下一個字的開頭音，只是 [w] 不要唸得太強（[w] 等於是「子音化」的 [u] 或 [ʊ]，分類上叫做「滑音」），例如：

◆　[u]

● you all ＝ youwall

你們都是

◆ [aʊ]

● how ugly ＝ howwugly

如此醜陋

◆ [oʊ]

● go on ＝ gowon

繼續

● so old ＝ sowold

如此老

● go away ＝ gowaway

走開

(2)

[j]滑音

當之前的單字的最後一個音是 [i] 或 [eɪ] 或 [aɪ] 或 [ɔɪ]時，下一個字要把 [j] 作為開頭音，只是 [j] 一樣不要唸得太強（[j] 等於是「子音化」的 [i] 或 [ɪ]，分類上也是個「滑音」），例如：

 track 003

◆ [i]

● we answered ＝ weyanswered
我們回答了

● He asked ＝ heyasked
他發問了

◆ [eɪ]

● say oh ＝ sayoh
說「噢」

◆ [aɪ]

● Thai app ＝ Thaiyapp
泰式應用軟體

◆ [ɔɪ]

● toy animal ＝ toyanimal
動物玩具

● boy attire ＝ boyattire
男孩裝扮

4. t & d 省音

　　字尾是t或d的字，後面接的字字首是子音時，t或d不發音。之所以會有這個口語消音規則產生，是因為在後面沒有母音的情況要將唸t和d唸出來很費力，所以自然而然地就將t和d給省略，這樣唸起來會比較快一點。

track 003

(1)字尾是t字，後面接的字字首是子音時：

例如：

● last chance → las chance
最後的機會

● most popular → mos popular
最受歡迎的

● most common → moscommon
最普通的

● most days → mos days
大部分日子

● next day → nex day
接下來的那天

● next month → nex month
下個月

● I don't know → I donno
我不知道

(2)字尾是d字，後面接的字字首是子音時：

● hand bag → han bag
手提包

 track 004

● hand made → han made
　手作的

5. h 省音

如果第二的單字的字首是 h 開頭又不是重音節的話，h 就會省略，母語者會直接用前一個字的字尾接續第二個字的母音。

● tell him → tellim
　告訴他

● tell her → teller
　告訴她

● let him → letim
　讓他

● let her → leter
　讓她

● get him → getim
　使他

6. 其它

(1) - t + you / -d + you

(a)以 t 結尾的字遇到 you 時，會變成 ch 的音，而原本的 t 不見了。

例如：

● meet you → meet'chu
遇見你

● can't you → can'chu
你不能

● got you → go'chu
使你

● catch you → ca'chu
抓到你

(b)以 d 結尾的字遇到 you 時，會變成 j 的音，而原本的 d 不見了。

● could you → coul'ju
你能否

● did you → di'ju
你曾經

(2)弱讀

口語中在非重讀音節會將母音弱讀成 [ə]，並快速唸過去。

(a) you 弱化母音 u 的部分唸成 [jə]。

track 005

例如：

● See you.→ see ya.
　再見

● What are you doing?→ wha [dər] ya doin'?
　你在做什麼？

(b) to 母音弱化成 [tə]

例如：

● have got to→gotta
　I have got to go.→ I gotta go→ gotta go
　我必須要離開了。

● going to→ gonna
　We are going to call you back.→ We are gonna call
　you back.
　我們會回你電話。

(c) of母音弱化成 [ə] 的音，當後面的字開頭是子音
時不發 f 的音，常和前面字的結尾子音行成連音。

例如：

● sort of → sorta
　有點

track 005

● kind of→ kinda

有些

● a lot of→ a lota

很多

● out of→ outa

離開

(d) for 母音弱化為 [ə]。

例如：

● Do it for your family.

為你的家庭做這件事。

(e) at母音弱化為 [ə]。

例如：

● Stay at home.

待在家裡。

● Nobody is looking at you.

沒有人在看你。

(3) and 簡化只剩下 'n' 的音

例如：

● rock and roll → rock 'n' roll

搖滾

 track 006

● fish and chips → fish 'n' chips
炸魚配薯條

(4) ing在發音時常省略g的音，只發成：in'

例如：

● What are you doin'?
你在做什麼？

● We are singin' and dancin'.
我們在唱歌跳舞。

● Stop laughin' at her.
別取笑她。

● They are makin' fun at him.
他們在捉弄他。

● 二、語調

　　語調指的是句子中的音調，也就是哪些部分該用重音來唸，通常用重音來唸的是最想強調的意思，也就是最想要聽者注意的部分，通常所有的實詞（名詞、動詞、形容詞、部份副詞）都是有重音的；虛詞（冠詞、連接詞、介係詞、代名詞、助動詞、be 動詞、部份副詞）則沒有重音。

track 006

實詞：名詞、動詞、形容詞、部份副詞

　　　例如：apple 蘋果, eat 吃, red 紅色的, carefully
　　　仔細地

虛詞：冠詞、連接詞、介係詞、代名詞、助動詞、be 動
　　　詞、部份副詞

　　　例如：a/an 一個, and 和, in 在, it 它, can 能,
　　　is 是, very 很

例句：

　　以下劃底線部分為實詞，需要用重音唸；其餘為虛
詞，不需要用重音唸。

例 This project took me about one year to complete
and it was a great success.
這個專案我花了大概一年完成，結果非常成功。

　　但是如果是已經提過一次以上的實詞，再度提到時，
就不需用重音唸，因為舊資訊對聽者來說，已經相對沒
有那麼重要了，重音通常會放在新資訊上面。

例句：

　　以下劃底線部分為要用重音唸的部分。

例 This is the restaurant we often went to when we
were students. The restaurant features Indian
curry.
這是我們學生時代常去的餐廳。這家餐廳主打印度
咖哩。

track 007

（第一句：the restaurant 第一次提到，需用重音唸；第二句：第二次提到 The restaurant，屬於已經知道的資訊，所以不要用重音唸）

有兩個以上的字詞相對比時，則要將重音放在要對比的字詞上，其餘的字都不要用重音唸，包含實詞，這是因為要凸顯所要對比的事物，所以將重音放在要對比的資訊上面。

例句：

以下劃底線部分為要用重音唸的部分。

例 The restaurant sells Tibetan cuisine, not Indian cuisine.

這家餐廳賣的是西藏料理，而不是印度料理。

（Tibetan cuisine 與 Indian cuisine 對比，所以要用重音唸，其餘的字都不要。）

附註：中文也有改變音調的情形，例如兩個三聲的字在一起，第一個三聲變成二聲：

例如：

「很」好
「很」早
蘋果的「鐵」粉「很」早就來排隊了。

● 三、聽音辨義

1. 多義字

很多單字有多個意思，所以要多注意重複出現的單字，經常是陷阱。

一字多義表

bank	銀行 [名]	河岸 [名]
book	書本 [名]	預定 [動]
change	改變 [名]、變成 [動]	零錢 [名]
charge	收費 [動]	指控 [動]
cool	涼快的 [形]	酷的 [形]
current	波浪 [名]	現在的 [形]
exercise	運動 [動]	練習題 [名]
fan	扇子 [名]	歌迷、影迷 [名]
floor	地板 [名]	樓層 [名]
foot	腳 [名]	英呎 [名]
key	鑰匙 [名]	用鍵盤輸入 [動]
kid	小孩 [名]	開玩笑 [動]
kind	種類 [名]	親切的 [形]
last	最後的 [形]	持續 [動]
lie	躺 [動]	說謊 [動]

track 008

park	公園 [名]	停車 [動]
play	戲劇 [名]	玩；演奏 [動]
poor	貧窮的 [形]	可憐的 [形]
room	房間 [名]	空間 [名]
ship	船 [名]	運送 [動]
shop	商店 [名]	購物 [動]
store	商店 [名]	貯存 [動]
table	桌子 [名]	表格 [名]
train	火車 [名]	訓練 [動]
watch	錶 [名]	觀看 [動]

2. 注意發音相似或相同的字

發音相似或相同的字常常會成為選項陷阱。

相似音表

相似音字組		解釋
aboard 登機	**abroad** 去國外	**aboard** 指的是登機、登船的意思，常聽到的用法是"**Welcome aboard**"；**abroad** 指的是去國外、在國外，例如：**go abroad**。
cancel 取消	**cancer** 癌症	**cancel** 經常出現在商用對話中，意思是取消，而**cancer** 指的是癌症，請仔細聽發音的差別。

track 008

card 卡片	**car** 車子	**card** 與 **car**，差別只有 **card** 最後多了一個音，講快的時候很容易沒有聽到，所以除了仔細聽之外，也要注意出現情境。
change 改變	**exchange** 交換	**exchange** 只比 **change** 前面多了 **ex**，都是無聲子音，要小心不要漏聽。
context 上下文	**contest** 比賽	**context** 意思是文章上下文；**contest** 是比賽、競賽，例如 **beauty contest** 選美比賽。
cooperate 合作	**corporate** 企業的	**cooperate** 在商業中常用，意思是合作，當動詞用；**corporate** 是企業的，是形容詞，例如 **corporate culture** 企業文化。
custom 習俗	**costume** 裝扮	**custom** 是習俗的意思；**costume** 是某一地方或時期的裝扮。
department 部門	**apartment** 公寓	這兩個單字都很基本，但是還是會有很多人在聽的時候弄混，通常多注意這兩個單字的出現場合，就不會出錯。
ear 耳	**year** 年	**year** 只比 **ear** 多了一個前面的滑音 [j]，可不要搞混了。
employer 雇主	**employee** 員工	這兩個字出自法文，動詞為 **employ** 雇用，加上 **-er** 表示雇用他人的人，加上 **-ee** 表示受雇的人。
fool 笨蛋	**full** 充滿的	**fool** 的母音為長音，**full** 的母音則為短音。
snake 蛇	**snack** 點心	這兩個字差別在於母音，**snake** 的母音是 [e]；**snack** 的母音是 [æ]。

 track 009

walk 走路	work 工作	這兩個簡單單字唸快了真的有點像，要注意了。
weekend 周末	weaken 使變弱	兩個字只有字尾 **d** 的差別，尤其是 **weaken** 變成過去分詞 **weakened**，又更像 **weekend**。
when 何時	where 何地	兩個字都出現在句首就更要注意了，因為搞混了，答案也就完全不同了。

相同音表

air 空氣	**heir** 繼承人
ant 螞蟻	**aunt** 父母的姊妹
ascent 上升	**assent** 同意
bare 光禿禿的	**bear** 熊
be 是	**bee** 蜜蜂
berry 漿果	**bury** 埋葬
bough 樹枝	**bow** 鞠躬
brake 煞車器	**break** 打破
capital 首都	**capitol** 美國州議會會址
carat 克拉	**carrot** 胡蘿蔔
cell 細胞	**sell** 賣
cereal 穀物做的食品	**serial** 連載小說
close 關閉	**clothes** 衣服

track 009

complement 補充物	**compliment** 稱讚
council 委員會	**counsel** 忠告
dear 親愛的	**deer** 鹿
desert 放棄	**dessert** 甜點
dew 露	**due** 應該付的
die 死亡	**dye** 染色
elusion 規避	**illusion** 幻覺
eye 眼睛	**I** 我
fair 公平的	**fare** 旅費
fairy 小仙子	**ferry** 乘船渡水
flea 跳蚤	**flee** 逃走
flour 麵粉	**flower** 花
foreword 序	**forward** 向前地
forth 向前	**fourth** 第四
hair 毛髮	**hare** 野兔
hear 聽	**here** 這裡
heroin 海洛英	**heroine** 女英雄
hour 小時	**our** 我們的
idle 懶惰的	**idol** 偶像
in 在	**inn** 小旅館
it's it is 的縮寫	**its it** 的所有格，它的
knight 騎士	**night** 黑夜
knot 打結	**not** 不
know 知道	**no** 不
mail 郵件	**male** 男性的
marry 結婚	**merry** 快樂的
meat 肉類	**meet** 相遇
miner 礦工	**minor** 次要的

none 毫無、無一人	nun 修女
one 一	won 贏
pea 豌豆	pee 小便
peak 尖端、頂點	peek 偷看
pedal 踏板	peddle 販賣
plain 平原	plane 飛機
pray 乞求	prey 獵物
principal 中小學校長	principle 信條
rap 銳聲說出	wrap 包起來
real 真的	reel 紡車
role 角色	roll 滾
root 根	route 路線
sail 航行	sale 銷售
sea 海	see 看
some 一些	sum 總和
son 兒子	sun 太陽
stair 階梯	stare 凝視
steal 偷	steel 鋼
tail 尾	tale 故事
sweet 糖果	suite 套房
toe 足趾	tow 拖吊
waist 腰部	waste 浪費
wait 等	weight 重量
ware 商品	wear 穿
wave 波浪；揮手	waive 放棄
way 路	weigh 稱重量
weak 虛弱	week 星期
yoke 牛軛；枷鎖	yolk 蛋黃

四、各國口音

新多益口音：美式（Am）、加拿大（Cn）、英式（Br）、澳洲（Aus）四種。

主要需要注意的是：美式發音（American English）vs. 英式發音（British English），因為加拿大發音近似美式發音，而澳洲發音近似加了鼻音的英式發音。

美式英語和英式英語若仔細區分，還真有許多不同：

1. 發音上差異

大抵來說，美式英語的語調相對平穩，聽起來每個詞語的調域變化小；而英式英語的發音強調重音與輕音，抑揚頓挫比較明顯。

大致而言，美式英語與英式英語差異如下：

(1) r 的發音

在美式英語中，r在字尾的捲舌音都會被強調出來，但在英式英語中通常不明顯或不見了。

例如：teacher 或 car 的音，在英國會被讀成聽起來像teacha 或 ca 的音。

(2) 非重讀的字母e

在美式英語中通常發音是 [ə]，在英式英語中讀為 [ɪ]except 在美國讀為 [ək`sɛpt]，在英國讀為 [ɪk`sɛpt]。

> 例如：difficult

(3) 有時 a 的音在美式英語中讀 [æ]，但在英式英語讀 [a]，例如 pass 和 ask 聽起來不一樣。

> 例如：after

(4) 有時 o 的音在美式英語中讀成 [a]，但在英式英語中讀成 [o]。例如 box 的讀法兩者就不同。

> 例如：pocket
> Impossible

(5) 美式英語會將t 重讀為 d，但英式英語則不會。

當 t 的音夾在兩個母音之間，前一個母音讀重音，後一個是輕音時，美國人習慣將 t 讀成 d 的音。

所以 writer（作家）的音讀起來就很像 rider（騎馬者），還有 latter（後者）與 ladder（梯子）美國讀音相同。

track 011

★ 讓我們來聽聽美式發音與英式發音的差異！

	美式英語 **American English**	英式英語 **British English**
(1)	**teacher** [ˋtitʃɚ] 老師 **car** [kɑr] 車	**teacher** [ˋtitʃə] 老師 **car** [kɑ] 車
(2)	**except** [əkˋsɛpt] 除了	**except** [ɪkˋsɛpt] 除了
(3)	**after** [ˋæftɚ] 之後 **pass** [pæs] 經過 **ask** [æsk] 詢問	**after** [ˋɑftə] 之後 **pass** [pɑs] 經過 **ask** [ɑsk] 詢問
(4)	**box** [bɑks] 盒子 **pocket** [ˋpɑkɪt] 口袋 **impossible** [ɪmˋpɑsəb!] 不可能	**box** [bɔks] 盒子 **pocket** [ˋpɔkɪt] 口袋 **impossible** [ɪmˋpɔsəb!] 不可能
(5)	**writer** [ˋraɪdɚ] 作家 **latter** [ˋlædɚ] 後者	**writer** [ˋraɪtə] 作家 **latter** [ˋlætə] 後者

2. 說話習慣不同

(1) 英國人愛用附加問句結尾，但美式英語比較少如此。
譬如，英國人很愛這麼說：

It's such a hot day, isn't it?

You haven't met her, have you?

(2)英國人愛用現在完成式，而美國人愛用過去式。

美式英語：She went to Tokyo before.

英式英語：She has been to Tokyo before.

美式英語：Did you find the bag?

英式英語：Have you found the bag?

(3) 英國人愛用動詞Have來開始問「是否有」，而美國人愛用助動詞do, does, did。

美式英語：Do you have the money?

英式英語：Have you the money?

3. 用詞上差異

　　用詞上美式與英式英語也有些差異，例如美式稱糖果為 candy，英式則是 lolly；美式稱購物手推車為 cart，英式則是 trolley；美式稱卡車為 truck，英式則是 lorry；美式稱毛衣為 sweater，英式則是 jumper；美式稱餅乾為 cookie，英式則是 biscuit。因為這裡主要在探討美式與英式英語於聽力上的差異，所以不一一詳述用詞上的不同。

　　只要平時多加留意美式英語和英式英語的差異，就不會有太大的理解問題。

五、英語生活化口語用法

很多英語生活化口語用法都很特別，並不是字面上的意思，而是另有弦外之音，下面列舉幾個供大家參考：

口語用法	中文意思	例句
You bet.	你說的沒錯	A：**Next time please make an appointment online to save time.** A：下次請用網路預約好節省時間。 B：**You bet.** B：你說的沒錯。
Tell me about it.	就是說啊！ 可不是嗎？	A：**That meeting was so boring.** A：那場會議真是無聊。 B：**Tell me about it.** B：可不是嗎？
Get lost!	滾開！	A：**You owe me an apology.** A：你欠我一個道歉。 B：**Get lost!** B：滾開！
way too	太過於……	A：**It is way too early to apply for the position now.** A：現在申請這個職缺太過早了。 B：**You are probably right.** B：或許你說的對。

pretty much	差不多	A：What kind of job are you looking for? A：你在找什麼樣的工作？ B：Pretty much anything. B：幾乎任何工作都可。
kind of sort of	有一點	A：What do you think of the new manager? A：你覺得新來的經理怎麼樣？ B：He is kind of weird. B：他有點奇怪。
nail it	搞定了	A：How did your report to the boss go? A：你向老闆的報告做得怎麼樣？ B：I nailed it. B：我搞定了。
Yeah, right.	最好是這樣啦	A：We'll give you a raise if you do the project well. A：如果你的專案做得好的話，我們會給你加薪。 B：Yeah, right. B：最好是這樣啦。
Absolutely! Totally! Exactly!	真的！ 是的！	A：Everyone should be on time for meetings in this company. A：公司開會時大家都要準時到。 B：Absolutely. B：是的！
Shut up! Get out! No way!	不可能吧！ 太扯了！ 少來！ 別鬧了！	A：Do you know Jason and Amy got married? A：你知道傑森和愛咪結婚了嗎？ B：Shut up! B：太扯了！

六、用情境來聯想單字

　　聽英文就像在讀英文，不需要字字句句都百分之百聽懂才能理解，重要的是要掌握關鍵字，以及由關鍵字延伸出來的字彙用法，建議在學習英文單字片語時，要留意對話或獨白的情境，學習時不要硬記，而是以「有劇情」的方式來聯想單字，並且分門別類來記憶，例如辦公室或海外出差等常用語，如此在聽力測驗或真實生活中，只要一聽到某些字詞，就會於腦中聯想起特定情境與一連串相關英語用法，這樣對於聽力和閱讀的理解，都會有非常大的幫助。

　　請特別注意下一章中 Part 3 & Part 4 依不同主題整匯的單字與用法，如果能夠花心思學習和善用，無論是於考場或職場都能無往不利。

New TOEIC

4

破解聽力各 Parts

track 014

LISTENING TEST

In the Listening test, you will be asked to demonstrate how well you understand spoken English. The entire Listening test will last approximately 45 minutes. There are four parts, and directions are given for each part. You must mark your answers on the separate answer sheet. Do not write your answers in your test book.

聽力測驗

在這個聽力測驗,你必須要展現你對口說英語的理解程度,整個聽力測驗大概會持續 45 分鐘,總共有四部分,每部分都會有解說,你必須要在另一張答案紙上作答,請不要在你的測驗本上寫答案。

總論:

所謂「知己知彼,百戰百勝」,在準備多益聽力測驗時,更要把握此原則,聽力分為4 Parts:

Part 1 看照片,選答案
Part 2 一問一答
Part 3 連續對話
Part 4 簡短獨白

　　無論在哪一Parts，一定要於播音之前先看題目，包含照片與圖片，還有題目與選項，就算是沒有時間看完所有題目與選項內容，也請務必看重點，也就是關鍵字，這樣在聽的時候，才好掌握住重點。

　　經常會考數字，例如日期、時間、價錢、折扣等等，在 Part 3 和 Part 4 的數字還常會與圖表同時出現，答案有時還需要綜合聽與讀，做些簡單演算。

　　新多益經常考多義字，還有相似音字和同音字，平時學習單字時必須要將其詞性變化與相關用法都一併記牢，特別有些單字名詞與動詞相同拼法，只是重音不同，如果沒有將這些發音細節都一併學好記牢的話，可能在聽到的時候，就會發生辨識的困難，造成聽力理解的挑戰。

　　改制後的新多益還常考的項目是日常口語常用的表達方式，如果沒有聽過這個用法，就要靠情境脈絡的上下文來推測，例如："get out (of here)" 字面上意思：離開這裡；引申意思：別開玩笑了；別鬧了。

　　以下就一一破解各個Part 的出題類型，並且提供平時準備與應考策略，還有常見情境的常見字彙與用法整理。

　　附註：

　　以下 (n.) 代表「名詞」；(v.) 代表「動詞」；(phr.) 代表「片語」

Part 1 照片描述

Directions : For each question in this part, you will hear four statements about a picture in your test book. When you hear the statements, you must select the one statement that best describes what you see in the picture. Then find the number of the question on your answer sheet and mark your answer. The statements will not be printed in your test book and will be spoken only one time.

解說：在這個部分的每一題，你都會聽到四個關於一張照片的描述，當你聽到這些描述時，必須要選出一個對你所看到照片的最佳描述，然後在答案紙上相對應的題號下劃記作答，這些描述不會在你的測驗本上印出來，而且只會播放一次。

範例

track 016

(A) They are moving some furniture.

(B) They are entering a meeting room.

(C) They are sitting at a table.

(D) They are cleaning the carpet.

(A) 他們正在搬傢俱。

(B) 他們正走進一間會議室。

(C) 他們正坐在一張桌子旁。

(D) 他們正在清理地毯。

Statement (C), "They're sitting at a table," is the best description of the picture, so you should select answer (C) and mark it on your answer sheet.

正確選項：(C)

解析：

(C) 選項：" 他們正坐在一張桌子旁 " 是描述這張照片的最佳選項，所以你應該要選 (C)，並且劃記在答案紙上。

1. 注意重點

還沒有播放問題與選項之前務必要先細看照片與選項。

注意：

(1) 注意照片中出現的人事物

如果是無人照片，請注意物品與環境之間的相對位置和狀態。

如果是有人照片，單人題請注意此人在什麼地方做什麼；多人題則除了注意這幾個人在什麼地方做什麼之外，還可能要比較外貌裝扮與動作異同。

(2) 注意相似音的陷阱

例如：poor 貧窮的 vs. pool 池；apartment 公寓 vs. department 部門。

(3) 注意有多種含意的單字或片語

例如：plant 可以是「工廠」，也可以是「植物」。

(4) 注意表示某樣東西存在的句子

There is⋯　（有）＋單數名詞
There are⋯　（有）＋複數名詞

(5) 注意表示位置或狀態的用語

介系詞 & 介系詞片語：

in 在, before 在⋯之前, in front of 在⋯之前, behind 在⋯之後, next to 在⋯旁邊, on top of 在⋯之上

例如：The man is standing in front of the information desk.

這個男子正站在服務台前。

(6) 注意表示動作或表示狀態的用語

現在簡單式被動例如：The car is parked.（車子停好了）

現在進行式被動例如：The car is being parked.（正在停車）

現在完成式被動例如：The car has been parked.（車子已經停好了）

2. 出題類型

照片情境

Unit 1 物品照片描述題

　　請於播放題目前先觀察照片，此類照片內沒有人物，請注意照片內物品的相對位置，留意描述此場景經常會出現的單字與用法。

　　以下照片皆無人在

一、會議室

例題：

◆ **Look at the picture on your test book.**

(A) This is a room for taking a break.

(B) This is a room for having a meeting.

(C) This is a room for heating up lunch.

(D) This is a room for doing photocopying.

track 018

中文翻譯：

◆ 看試題冊上的這張照片。

(A) 這是間用來放鬆的房間。

(B) 這是間用來開會的房間。

(C) 這是間用來加熱午餐的房間。

(D) 這是間用來影印的房間。

正確選項：B

(1) 聽寫

1. There are four ⬛⬛⬛ in the room.

2. There is a keyboard on the ⬛⬛⬛.

3. All seats are ⬛⬛⬛.

4. There is a ⬛⬛⬛ pot in the room.

空格

1. chairs

2. desk

3. unoccupied

4. plant

翻譯

1. 在這個房間有 4 張椅子。

2. 在這張桌子上有 1 個鍵盤。

3. 所有的座位都空著。

4. 在這間房間有個盆栽。

track 018

(2) 跟讀

It is a newly furnished meeting room.
這是間剛裝潢好的會議室。

The windows of the room are made of frosted glass.
這間房間的窗戶是用毛玻璃做的。

In front of the supervisor's chair, there are three seats.
在主管位子前有 3 張椅子。

All seats are now empty.
現在所有的椅子都空著。

The lights are all turned on.
所有的燈都是亮著的。

A picture is displayed on a wall.
一張照片被展示在牆上。

(3) 會議室注意事項

描述空會議室常會出現的字彙&片語：

equip (v.)	配備
fully furbished (phr.)	裝潢完整的
furnish (v.)	裝潢
newly furnished (phr.)	全新裝潢的
newly refurbished (phr.)	全新裝潢的

track 019

newly renovated (phr.)	全新整修的
occupied (adj.)	有人使用的相反詞：
	unoccupied (adj.) 無人使用的
projector (n.)	投影機
screen (n.)	投影機布幕
seat(n.)	位置

二、客服中心

例題：

◆ **Look at the picture on your test book.**

(A) Workers test samples here.

(B) Editors busy working on texts here.

(C) Staff package products here.

(D) Customer service clerks contact clients here.

track 019

中文翻譯：

◆ 看試題冊上的這張照片。

(A) 工人在這裡測試樣品。

(B) 編輯在這裡忙著看稿件。

(C) 員工在這裡包裝產品。

(D) 客服人員在這裡聯絡客戶。

正確選項：D

(1) 聽寫

1. There are rows of ______ in the room.
2. There are two ______ in one cubicle.
3. ______ is currently in the customer service room.
4. A ______ is hung next to the computer.

空格

1. cubicles
2. seats
3. Nobody
4. headphone

翻譯

1. 在這間房間內有一排排的辦公室隔間。
2. 每間辦公室隔間有兩個座位。
3. 現在沒有人在客服室內。
4. 一個頭戴耳機掛於電腦旁。

 track 020

(2) 跟讀

There are many rows of customer service cubicles.
這裡有很多列的客服隔間。

In each cubicle there are two seats.
每個隔間內有兩個座位。

The headphones are hung next to the desks.
頭戴耳機掛於桌子旁。

At the moment all monitors of the desktop computers are shut down.
現在所有螢幕都關了。

(3) 客服中心注意事項

描述空客服中心常會出現的字彙&片語：

answer e-mails (phr.)	回覆電子郵件
complaint (n.)	抱怨
cubicle (n.)	辦公室小隔間
customer service (phr.)	客戶服務
customer service clerk (phr.)	客戶服務專員
headphone (n.)	頭戴式耳機
microphone (n.)	麥克風
take phone calls (phr.)	接聽來電

三、個人辦公室

例題：

◆ **Look at the picture on your test book.**

(A) This looks like a tea room.

(B) This looks like a reception's area.

(C) This looks like a supervisor's office room.

(D) This looks like a private living room.

中文翻譯：

◆ 看試題冊上的這張照片。

(A) 這間房間看來是茶室。

(B) 這間房間看來是接待區。

(C) 這間房間看來是主管辦公室。

(D) 這間房間看來是私人臥室。

正確選項：C

(1) 聽寫

1. There are ▮▮▮▮ chairs in the room.
2. There is a ▮▮▮▮ on the desk.
3. All chairs are ▮▮▮▮.
4. The windows are covered by ▮▮▮▮.

空格

1. three
2. telephone
3. unoccupied
4. blinds

翻譯

1. 房間內有三張椅子。
2. 桌子上有個電話。
3. 所有的椅子都是空的。
4. 窗戶有百葉窗蓋著。

(2) 跟讀

It is an office room.
這是間辦公室。

Nothing except a telephone is on the desk.
桌上只有一個電話。

track 021

There are two seats in front of the desk.
桌前有兩個座位。

All seats are now unoccupied.
所有的座位現在都空著。

(3) 辦公室注意事項

描述空辦公室常會出現的字彙&片語：

blinds (n.)	百葉窗
bulk (n.)	大量
drawer (n.)	抽屜
empty (adj.)	空的
folder (n.)	資料夾
plenty (adj.)	多的
space (n.)	空間
stationery (n.)	文具

四、接待室

例題：

 track 022

◆ **Look at the picture on your test book.**

(A) This looks like a reception's room.

(B) This looks like a library.

(C) This looks like a storage room.

(D) This looks like a bedroom.

中文翻譯：

◆ 看試題冊上的這張照片。

(A) 這間房間看來是接待室。

(B) 這間房間看來是照片書館。

(C) 這間房間看來是儲藏室。

(D) 這間房間看來是臥室。

正確選項：A

(1) 聽寫

1. There are four ▨ in the reception room.

2. There are three ▨ on the sofas.

3. One plant ▨ is in the room.

4. The windows are covered by ▨.

空格

1. sofas

2. cushions

3. pot

4. curtains

翻譯

1. 接待室有 4 張沙發。

2. 沙發上有 3 個靠墊。

3. 房間內有一盆栽。

4. 窗戶有窗簾蓋著。

(2) 跟讀

It is a reception room.
這是間接待室。

It looks very cozy.
這裡看來很舒適。

The cushions on the sofas looks comfortable.
沙發上的靠墊看來很舒服。

All seats are now unoccupied.
所有座位現在都空著。

(3) 接待室注意事項

描述空接待室常會出現的字彙&片語：

beverage (n.)	飲品
couch (n.)	沙發，長椅
cozy (adj.)	舒服的
drink (n.)	飲料
reception (n.)	接待
reception desk (phr.)	服務台
receptionist (n.)	接待員

track 023

refreshment (n.)	茶點，便餐；飲料
registration (n.)	登記
sofa (n.)	沙發
switchboard girl/boy (n.)	總機小姐／先生

五、茶水間

例題：

◆ **Look at the picture on your test book.**

(A) This looks like a toilet room.

(B) This looks like a tea room.

(C) This looks like a meeting room.

(D) This looks like a photocopy room.

track 023

中文翻譯：

◆ 看試題冊上的這張照片。

(A) 這間房間看來是廁所。

(B) 這間房間看來是茶水間。

(C) 這間房間看來是會議室。

(D) 這間房間看來是影印室。

正確選項：B

(1) 聽寫

1. There is a dish ▨▨▨ in the tea room.

2. There is a microwave ▨▨▨ on the cabinet.

3. The ▨▨▨ is quite clean.

4. The ▨▨▨ purifier stands against the wall.

- -

空格

1. washer

2. oven

3. sink

4. water

翻譯

1. 茶水間內有個洗碗機。

2. 櫥櫃上有個微波爐。

3. 流理台蠻乾淨的。

4. 靠牆的地方有個淨水器。

(2) 跟讀

It is a tea room in an office.
辦公室內有個茶水間。

There are tea bags in the drawer.
抽屜內有茶包。

Many staff members come to this tea room to take a break.
很多員工到這間茶水間來休息。

This tea room is maintained very much in order.
這間茶水間維持得很整齊。

(3) 茶水間注意事項

描述空茶水間常會出現的字彙&片語：

cabinet (n.)	壁櫥
coffee machine (n.)	咖啡機
dish washer (n.)	洗碗機
kitchen towel (n.)	抹布
microwave oven (n.)	微波爐
sink (n.)	洗手台
water filter/purifier (n.)	淨水器

六、飯店房間

例題：

◆ **Look at the picture on your test book.**

  (A) This looks like a room in a five-star hotel.

  (B) This looks like a small meeting room.

  (C) This looks like a maintenance room.

  (D) This looks like an exhibition room.

中文翻譯：

◆ 看試題冊上的這張照片。

  (A) 這間房間看起來像是五星級飯店的房間。

  (B) 這間房間看起來像是間小型會議室。

  (C) 這間房間看起來像是維修室。

  (D) 這間房間看來像是展示間。

正確選項：A

track 025

(1) 聽寫

1. There is a ▮▮▮▮▮ table in the hotel room.
2. There is a ▮▮▮▮▮ table next to the sofa.
3. The yellow ▮▮▮▮▮ looks like a bed.
4. The table ▮▮▮▮▮ next to the bed is soft.

- -

空格

1. bedside
2. coffee
3. sofa
4. light

翻譯

1. 這間飯店房間內有張床邊桌子。
2. 沙發旁有張咖啡桌。
3. 這張黃色沙發看來像張床。
4. 床邊的桌燈非常溫和。

(2) 跟讀

The curtains of the hotel room are shup up.
這間飯店房間的窗簾是關著的。

The view of the hotel room is amazing.
這間飯店房間的景觀很好看。

track 025

The hotel room is suitable for a couple.
這間飯店房間很適合夫妻情侶。

The hotel room comes with a huge space for receiving guests.
這間飯店房間有很寬敞的接待客人區。

(3) 旅館房間注意事項

描述空旅館房間常會出現的字彙&片語：

bathroom (n.)	廁所
booking (n.)	訂位
children's bed (n.)	小孩床位
concierge (n.)	旅館服務臺職員
reservation (n.)	訂位
sheet (n.)	床單

旅館房型如下：

double bed room	標準雙人房，也叫雙床房
single bed room	大床房，房間內設有一張可供兩個人睡的大床
twin bed room	單人房，房間內只有一張小床

 track 026

七、展場

例題：

◆ **Look at the picture on your test book.**

(A) This is a garage sale.

(B) This is a computer factory.

(C) This is a laptop exhibition room.

(D) This is a laptop repair shop.

中文翻譯：

◆ 看試題冊上的這張照片。

(A) 這是車庫大拍賣。

(B) 這是電腦工廠。

(C) 這是筆電展示間。

(D) 這是電腦維修廠。

正確選項：C

track 026

(1) 聽寫

1. There are many laptops on ▮▮▮▮▮.
2. There is a ▮▮▮▮▮ on some laptops.
3. The are many ▮▮▮▮▮ of laptops here.
4. The laptops seem to be on ▮▮▮▮▮.

空格

1. display
2. badge
3. rows
4. sale

翻譯

1. 這裡有很多筆電展示。
2. 有些筆電上有標籤。
3. 這裡有很多列筆電。
4. 這裡有很多筆電在特價拍賣中。

(2) 跟讀

The laptops on display are brand new.
展示中的筆電是全新的。

There are special sales on some laptops.
有些筆電在特價拍賣中。

track 026

The room is full of new laptops.
這間房間裡都是新筆電。

Many laptops of various brands are shown here.
這裡有各種不同牌子的筆電展示。

(3) 展場注意事項

描述無人展場常會出現的字彙&片語：

booth (n.)	貨攤
entrance (n.)	入口
exit (n.)	出口
information desk (n.)	服務台
on display (phr.)	展示中
self-help desk (n.)	自助服務台
stall (n.)	攤子
stand (n.)	攤位
ticket booth (n.)	售票亭
traffic flow (n.)	參觀人數／訪客流量
visitor route (n.)	參觀動線

八、餐廳

例題：

◆ **Look at the picture on your test book.**

(A) This is in a fast food store.

(B) This is a food display in a bistro.

(C) This is in a food stall.

(D) This is a set table in a restaurant.

中文翻譯：

◆ 看試題冊上的這張照片。

(A) 這是間速食店。

(B) 這是在快餐店裡的食品展示。

(C) 這是在美食攤內。

(D) 這是在餐廳裡擺飾好的餐桌。

正確選項：D

(1) 聽寫

1. The dining table is _____.

2. The _____ on the table looks very fine.

3. The _____ are neatly folded.

4. There is beautiful flower _____ on the table.

空格

1. set

2. silverware

3. napkins

4. arrangement

翻譯

1. 這張餐桌已經擺好餐具。

2. 這張餐桌上的銀製器具看起來很精緻。

3. 餐巾摺得很整齊。

4. 餐桌上有美麗花飾。

(2) 跟讀

Someone set the dining table with silverware.
有人已經在餐桌上擺好了銀製餐具。

It looks that western meals are going to be served.
看來是要上西餐了。

track 027

There are neat napkins on the plates.
盤子上有整齊的餐巾。

A candle will be lighted when the meal starts.
開動前會點蠟燭。

Many glasses are on the dining table.
餐桌上有很多玻璃杯。

There is one candle stand in the center of the table.
餐桌中央有個蠟燭台。

(3) 餐廳注意事項

描述餐廳常會出現的字彙&片語：

delicacy (n.)	美食，佳餚
dessert (n.)	點心
dining table (n.)	餐桌
high-end (adj.)	高檔的
main course (n.)	主菜
napkin (n.)	餐巾紙
set the table (phr.)	擺飯桌，擺餐具
side dish (n.)	小菜
tableware (n.)	餐具

 track 028

九、自動化工廠

例題：

◆ **Look at the picture on your test book.**

    (A) The automatic machines are applied in this factory.

    (B) Many people will lose their jobs due to machines.

    (C) Humans work more efficiently than machines.

    (D) Many automatic machines are not safe.

中文翻譯：

◆ 看試題冊上的這張照片。

    (A) 這間工廠裡有很多自動機器。

    (B) 很多人因為機器而失去工作。

    (C) 人類比機器有工作效率。

    (D) 很多自動機器不安全。

正確選項：A

track 028

(1) 聽寫

1. Factories are equipped with ▓▓▓▓ machines.

2. ▓▓▓▓ has become quite popular these days.

3. Humans have to work ▓▓▓▓ with machines.

4. Automatizationis the goal for most ▓▓▓ industries.

空格

1. automatic

2. Artificial intelligence

3. side by side

4. manufacturing

翻譯

1. 工廠裡有很多自動機器。

2. 人工智慧最近變得很風行。

3. 人類必須跟機器肩並肩工作。

4. 自動化是製造業的目標。

(2) 跟讀

AI has helped production lines tremendously in factories.

在工廠裡人工智慧對生產線有很大的助益。

 track 029

Automatic machines can do dangerous work done by humans before.
自動化機器能取代之前由人類來做的危險工作。

IT management helps monitor the production.
資訊科技幫助監控生產。

The Big Data can be gathered and analyzed.
可以蒐集並分析大數據。

(3) 自動化工廠注意事項

描述餐廳常會出現的字彙&片語：

AI = Artificial Intelligence (n.)	
	人工智慧
automatic (adj.)	自動的
automatization (n.)	自動化
drone (n.)	無人機
IT = Information Technology (n.)	
	資訊科技
production rate (n.)	生產率
productivity (n.)	生產力

track 029

十、停車場

例題：

◆ **Look at the picture on your test book.**

(A) There is a security guy here.

(B) Many people park their cars here more than 24 hours.

(C) Many cars are parked here.

(D) It is not a secure place to park your car.

中文翻譯：

看試題冊上的這張照片。

(A) 這裡有個保全。

(B) 很多人在這裡停車超過24小時。

(C) 這裡停了很多車子。

(D) 這裡不是安全的停車處。

正確選項：C

(1) 聽寫

1. This ▨▨▨ lot opens 24 hours.

2. ▨▨▨ a parking space is quite hardin this city these days.

3. No security guys are needed in this parking building because of theautomatic parking ▨▨▨ .

4. Customers of this wholesale store do not have to pay parking ▨▨▨ .

空格

1. parking

2. Finding

3. machine

4. fees

翻譯

1. 這停車場24小時開放。

2. 要在這個城市裡找停車位非常不容易。

3. 這棟停車大樓不需要保全人員，因為有自動停車收費機。

4. 這家量販店的顧客不需要付停車費。

track 030

(2) 跟讀

It is very hard to find a parking space during rush hours.
交通尖峰時間找停車位很困難。

Few companies have their own parking spots.
很少公司有自己的停車位。

Some people park their cars in the parking spaces of a wholesale store.
有些人在量販店的停車場停車。

Due to parking problems, many commuters choose public transportation instead.
因為停車問題，很多通勤者改選大眾交通工具。

Some people forget where they park after they come back.
有的人回來後忘記車子停在哪裡。

(3) 停車場注意事項

描述無人停車場常會出現的字彙&片語：

car route (n.)	行車路線
gate (n.)	閘門
occupied (adj.)	有人使用的相反詞：unoccu-pied (adj.) 無人使用的
parking lot (n.)	停車位
parking machine (n.)	停車收費機
parking space (n.)	停車位

 track 031

十一、工地

例題：

◆ **Look at the picture on your test book.**

(A) The security of building workers is taken care of.

(B) It will be a skyscraper in the downtown area.

(C) This is a dangerous construction site.

(D) A building is under construction here.

中文翻譯：

◆ 看試題冊上的這張照片。

(A) 這裡的工安做得很好。

(B) 在市中心會有座摩天高樓。

(C) 這是個危險的工地。

(D) 一棟建築物在施工中。

正確選項：D

(1) 聽寫

1. A _____ is working right now.

2. There are at least three _____ built.

3. No building workers are on _____ site now.

4. The building seems to be _____.

空格

1. crane

2. floors

3. construction

4. rectangular

翻譯

1. 起重機現在正在運作。

2. 那裡至少蓋有 3 層樓。

3. 現在工地沒有建築工人。

4. 這棟建築物似乎是長方形的。

(2) 跟讀

We can see a construction site in the picture.
我們可以看見照片裡的工地。

 track 032

There are at least three floors of the building.
這棟建築物至少有 3 層樓。

There is a crane on the right of the picture.
照片的右邊有個起重機。

There is no building worker in the picture.
照片中沒有建築工人。

(3) 工地注意事項

描述無人工地常會出現的字彙&片語：

building (n.)	建築物
construction site (n.)	建築工地
crane (n.)	起重機，吊車
drill (n.)	鑽機
equipment (n.)	設備
foreman (n.)	工頭
height (n.)	高度
security (n.)	安全
worker (n.)	工人

十二、傳真機

例題：

◆ **Look at the picture on your test book.**

(A) Some documents are being copied here.

(B) There is a fax machine in the room.

(C) There are several employees in the room.

(D) It is not clean on the ground.

中文翻譯：

◆ 看試題冊上的這張照片。

(A) 有些文件正在複印中。

(B) 在房間內有個傳真機。

(C) 在房間內有幾個員工。

(D) 地板不乾淨。

正確選項：B

track 033

(1) 聽寫

1. It is a place to fax and copy ▆▆▆▆.
2. The fax machine is ▆▆▆▆.
3. Employees can come in and fax ▆▆▆▆ they need to.
4. There is a trash can ▆▆▆▆ the fax machine.

空格

1. documents
2. turned on
3. whenever
4. next to

翻譯

1. 這是傳真、複印文件的地方。
2. 傳真機是開著的。
3. 員工可以在任何需要的時間進來傳真。
4. 傳真機旁有個垃圾桶。

(2) 跟讀

The new staff members have to learn to use the fax machine properly.
新進員工必須要學習正確使用傳真機的方法。

track 033

Some companies prefer sending fax to using e-mail.
有些公司偏愛使用傳真，不喜歡用電子郵件。

Check out the fax numbers first before using the fax machine.
使用傳真前要先查傳真號碼。

With this fax machine, you can also photocopy documents.
有了這台傳真機，你也可以影印文件。

(3) 傳真機注意事項

描述無人操作的傳真機常會出現的字彙&片語：

beep tone (n.)	嗶聲
bottom (n.)	底部
drawer (n.)	抽屜
maintenance (n.)	維修
office supply (n.)	辦公室用品
paper recycling (n.)	廢紙回收
paper tray (n.)	紙盒
run out of (phr.)	用完
space (n.)	空間
technician (n.)	技術員，技師
use up (phr.)	用盡

track 034

Unit 2 照片中有人物（單人／多人）

　　請於播放題目前先觀察照片，如果照片內出現一個人物，請先觀察此人裝扮與此人正在進行的動作，在心中預想描述這個人可能出現的英語用法；如果照片內出現多人，請先比較這些人裝扮與動作的異同，以及與情境的關係。

一、一男子在操作機器

例題：

◆ **Look at the picture on your test book.**

(A) The machine is out of order.

(B) The man is operating the machine.

(C) The machine can speak three languages.

(D) The man is capable of assembling the machine.

track 034

中文翻譯：

◆ 看試題冊上的這張照片。

(A) 這台機器壞了。

(B) 這個男子在操作機器。

(C) 這機器能說三種語言。

(D) 這個男子能組合機器。

正確選項：B

(1) 聽寫

1. He is the man in [____] of the whole factory.

2. The [____] control of this printing company is very well-known.

3. Workers on the [____] lines are concentrating on putting pieces of the toys together.

4. The machine does not [____] to the order of the computer.

空格

1. charge

2. quality

3. assembly

4. respond

track 035

翻譯

1. 他掌管這整間工廠。
2. 這間印刷廠的品質很出名。
3. 生產線上的工人正專注於將玩具組裝起來。
4. 這台機器對電腦指令沒反應。

(2) 跟讀

The technician in front of the machine looks confused.
機器前的技術工人看來困擾。

The machine seems to be out of order.
機器似乎壞了。

The factory does not have good ventilation so workers feel hot.
工廠沒有空調，所以工人感到很熱。

The workers on the assembly line all wear bunny suits.
生產線上的工人都穿著連身無塵衣。

The supervisor came to inspect with cleanroom suit.
主管穿著無塵衣進來檢查。

The guy who operates the machine does not know how that machine works.
操作這機器的男子不清楚那台機器如何運作。

(3) 工廠操作機器注意事項

描述工人於工廠操作機器常會出現的字彙&片語：

assembly line (n.)	生產線
be in order (phr.)	上軌道
bunny suit/cleanroom suit (n.)	無塵衣
function (n.)	功能
in charge of (phr.)	負責
operate (v.)	運作
out of order (phr.)	亂了秩序
quality control (n.)	品質管理
respond to (phr.)	回應
response (n.)	回覆
work performance (n.)	工作表現

二、簡報

例題：

◆ **Look at the picture on your test book.**

(A) The listeners do not like the man's presentation.

(B) The man is not well prepared.

(C) There is a flow chart on display.

(D) The presentation is about a company.

中文翻譯：

◆ 看試題冊上的這張照片。

(A) 聽眾不喜歡這男子的簡報。

(B) 這男子準備不周全。

(C) 有張流程照片在展示中。

(D) 這是關於一間公司的簡報。

正確選項：C

(1) 聽寫

1. The man is doing a ▨▨▨ in English.

2. The presentation is about the yearly ▨▨▨ of the department.

3. The presenter has prepared many ▨▨▨ aids.

4. The ▨▨▨ is listening to his presentation with interest.

空格

1. presentation

2. budget

3. visual

4. audience

track 036

翻譯

1. 這個男子正在用英語做簡報。

2. 這是關於年度部門經費的簡報。

3. 簡報者準備了很多視覺輔助。

4. 觀眾很感興趣地聽著他的簡報。

(2) 跟讀

The screen in front of the audience is very huge.
在觀眾前的螢幕非常大。

The man doing the presentation is speaking to a microphone.
在做簡報的這個男子正透過麥可風說話。

There are many charts in the presentation.
簡報中有很多照片表。

The presentation is about the process of integration of two departments.
這個簡報是關於兩個部門的整合過程。

(3) 簡報注意事項

描述簡報常會出現的字彙&片語：

attention (n.)	注意力
chart (n.)	圖表
feedback (n.)	回饋
flow chart (n.)	流程圖

track 037

focus(n. v.)	焦點
projector (n.)	投影機
projector screen (n.)	投影機螢幕
visual aid (n.)	視覺輔助

三、工人於工地

例題：

◆ **Look at the picture on your test book.**

(A) The workers are doing nothing much.

(B) The construction they are building is not stable.

(C) The two workers are not experienced.

(D) Two workers are working on the construction site.

track 037

中文翻譯：

◆ 看試題冊上的這張照片。

(A) 工人沒有什麼事做。

(B) 他們在蓋的建築物不穩固。

(C) 這兩個工人缺乏經驗。

(D) 有兩個工人在工地工作。

正確選項：D

(1) 聽寫

1. There is a ▨▨▨▨ crane in front of the workers.
2. The ▨▨▨▨ is giving orders to the workers.
3. Many new buildings in this ▨▨▨▨ are under construction.
4. ▨▨▨▨ on construction site is generally very expensive.

空格

1. giant
2. foreman
3. neighborhood
4. Equipment

翻譯

1. 在工人前面有一個巨大的起重機。
2. 工頭正在給工人下指令。

3. 這附近有很多新建築物在施工中。

4. 建築工地的器材通常都很貴。

(2) 跟讀

The workers are wearing helmets.
工人戴著安全帽。

Two workers are working on the construction site.
兩個工人正在建築工地工作著。

There seems to be little protection for the workers.
這些工人似乎沒有什麼安全保障。

What do you think is being built over there?
你想那邊在蓋什麼？

(3) 工人於工地注意事項

描述工人於工地常會出現的字彙&片語：

construction time (n.)	營建時間
labor (n.)	勞力
laborer (n.)	勞工
manual (adj.)	體力的
manual work (n.)	勞力的工作
transport (v.)	運輸
wage (n.)（尤指支付給體力勞動者的）工資	
working hour (n.)	工時

track 038

四、討論文件

例題：

◆ **Look at the picture on your test book.**

(A) They seem to be happily talking about a document.

(B) They do not want to have a discussion together.

(C) The woman is not patient with the man.

(D) The woman is correcting the man's report.

中文翻譯：

看試題冊上的這張照片。

(A) 他們似乎很愉快地討論一份文件。

(B) 他們不想要在一起討論。

(C) 女子對男子沒有耐心。

(D) 女子在修改男子的報告。

正確選項：A

track 039

(1) 聽寫

1. The man _____ a document to the woman.

2. They take every _____ into consideration.

3. You can _____ down project into 5 parts.

4. I am sure I am the most capable person for this _____ _____ .

空格

1. handed
2. point
3. break
4. task

翻譯

1. 這男子將一份文件交給這女子。

2. 他們將每個重點都列入考慮。

3. 你可以將這個專案分為 5 部分。

4. 我確定自己是最能勝任這個任務的人。

(2) 跟讀

They are discussing a document in an office.
他們正在辦公室討論文件。

They seem to disagree with each other about a matter.
他們似乎對一件事不同意。

track 039

The two employees are talking about a rundown.
這兩個員工在討論一個流程表。

They have reached agreement in the end of discussion.
討論結束後他們得到了共識。

We agree to disagree about this issue.
我們同意各人有各人看法。

(3) 同事討論文件注意事項

描述同事討論文件常會出現的字彙&片語：

approval (n.)	認可
argument (n.)	爭論
break down (phr.)	分解步驟
consideration (n.)	考量
disagreement (n.)	意見不同
discussion (n.)	討論
document (n.)	文件
issue (n.)	問題，爭議
point of view (phr.)	觀點
project (n.)	專案
task (n.)	任務

五、一個科學家在實驗室做實驗

例題：

◆ **Look at the picture on your test book.**

(A) The woman must be a doctor.

(B) The woman is a magician.

(C) The woman is doing tests in the lab.

(D) The woman is taking blood.

中文翻譯：

◆ 看試題冊上的這張照片。

(A) 這女子一定是位醫師。

(B) 這女子是位魔術師。

(C) 這女子在實驗室裡做測試。

(D) 這女子在抽血。

正確選項：C

track 040

(1) 聽寫

1. The safety of our products is ▓▓▓▓ before they are put on the market

2. Certificates are awarded after the toys get ▓▓▓▓ of safety standards regulations.

3. The subject shows no response to the ▓▓▓▓ .

4. Scientists should ▓▓▓▓ protection equipment when they conduct an experiment in the lab.

空格

1. tested
2. approval
3. stimulus
4. wear

翻譯

1. 我們產品安全於上市前經過測試。
2. 通過安全法規後的玩具可以獲得認證。
3. 受試者對刺激沒有反應。
4. 科學家於實驗室做實驗時應該要穿戴安全配備。

(2) 跟讀

We are glad that you have your own laboratory.
我們為你有自己的實驗室而高興。

The scientist is conducting an experiment in the lab.
科學家正在實驗室做實驗。

Most experiments are now carried out by computers.
現在大部分的實驗是由電腦操作的。

One has to be especially careful in a chemical lab.
在化學實驗室要特別小心。

(3) 在實驗室做實驗注意事項

描述在實驗室做實驗常會出現的字彙&片語：

alcohol (n.)	酒精
assistant (n.)	助理
carry out an experiment (phr.)	進行實驗
laboratory ＝ lab (n.)	實驗室
lab equipment (n.)	實驗室器材
test (v.)	測試
test tube (n.)	試管
trial and error (phr.)	反覆試驗

track 041

六、一個醫生正在看診間與一個病人談話

例題：

◆ **Look at the picture on your test book.**

(A) A woman is having her blood taken by a nurse.

(B) A woman is talking about her symptoms to a doctor.

(C) A woman is having her temperature taken by a nurse.

(D) A woman is selling something to the other woman.

track 042

中文翻譯：

看試題冊上的這張照片。

(A) 一女子正讓一位護理師抽血。

(B) 一女子正在向一醫師描述症狀。

(C) 一女子正讓一護理師量體溫。

(D) 一女子正在賣東西給另一女子。

正確選項：B

(1) 聽寫

1. Each patient has very ______ time talking to the doctor.
2. Patients are ______ to write down their questions before seeing a doctor.
3. ______ are important to people of all ages, especially the elderly.
4. Work-life ______ is vital to one's mental and physical health.

空格

1. limited
2. advised
3. Health check-ups
4. balance

track 042

翻譯

1. 每個病人與醫師的談話都很有限。

2. 我們建議病人於見醫師之前寫下問題。

3. 健康檢查對各年齡層的人都重要，特別是對年長者。

4. 工作生活平衡對一個人的身心健康很重要。

(2) 跟讀

The doctor called the nurse for assistance.
醫師請護理師協助。

The patient described his symptoms to the doctor.
病人向醫師描述他的症狀。

The patient came into the examining room in wheelchair.
病人坐著輪椅進入診間。

All patients should weigh on the scale and have their blood pressure taken before seeing the doctor.
所有病人必須於見醫師前量體重與體溫。

track 043

(3) 在看診間注意事項

描述在看診間常會出現的字彙&片語：

bandages (n.)	繃帶
band-aid (n.)	ＯＫ繃
blood pressure monitor (n.)	血壓計
cotton balls (n.)	棉花球
crutches (n.)	拐杖
examination (n.)	檢查
far infrared ray (n.)	遠紅外線
gauze (n.)	薄紗，網紗
ice pack (n.)	冰袋
injection (n.)	注射
physical therapy (n.)	物理療法
prescription (n.)	處方
surgery (n.)	外科醫學
syringe (n.)	注射器
thermometer (n.)	溫度計
wheelchair (n.)	輪椅

常見醫師名稱：

cardiologist	心臟病科醫師
dentist	牙醫
gynecologist	婦科醫師
obstetrician	產科醫師
optometrist	驗光師
pediatrician	小兒科醫師
psychiatrist	精神科醫師
surgeon	外科醫生

track 043

七、收銀員在結帳

例題：

◆ **Look at the picture on your test book.**

(A) The woman is scanning the bar codes of the items.

(B) The man is paying in credit card.

(C) The woman is checking the quality of the products.

(D) The man is looking for a missed tool.

中文翻譯：

◆ 看試題冊上的這張照片。

(A) 這女子正在掃描商品的磁條。

(B) 這男子正在用信用卡付費。

(C) 這女子正在檢查產品的品質。

(D) 這男子正在尋找遺失的工具。

正確選項：A

track 044

(1) 聽寫

1. The supermarket has a system of _____ .

2. The wholesale store has all _____ of products one can think of.

3. Most people buy in huge _____ in a wholesale store.

4. Customers can return the goods with _____ .

空格

   1. membership

   2. sorts

   3. quantity

   4. receipts

翻譯

   1. 這家超市採會員制。

   2. 量販店有各種你想得到的產品。

   3. 在量販店大部分人採購大量的商品。

   4. 顧客能憑收據來退貨。

(2) 跟讀

There is currently a special sale at that newly opened supermarket.
現在那家新開的超市有特價。

Customers can take time shopping and browsing through the aisles.
顧客可以慢慢採購，瀏覽各排商品。

This supermarket is famous for meat and dairy products from the States.
這家超市以美國進口的肉類與蛋奶類產品著名。

Customers can return the products in seven days after the purchase is done.
顧客可以在結帳 7 天內來退貨。

(3) 在超市注意事項

描述人在超市常會出現的字彙&片語：

cart (n.)	手推車
purchase (v.)	購買
quality (n.)	品質
quantity(n.)	數量
receipt(n.)	收據
retail shop(n.)	零售商
return policy(n.)	退貨規定
scanning(n.)	掃描
transaction(n.)	交易
wholesale store(n.)	大型賣場

 track 045

八、兩個人正一邊注視著電腦銀幕一邊討論

例題：

◆ Look at the picture on your test book.

(A) The two men are signing a contract.

(B) The two men are watching TV.

(C) The two men are looking at the screen.

(D) The two men are doing a deal.

中文翻譯：

◆ 看試題冊上的這張照片。

(A) 這兩個男子正在簽合約。

(B) 這兩個男子正在看電視。

(C) 這兩個男子正盯著螢幕看。

(D) 這兩個男子正在交易。

track 045

正確選項：C

(1) 聽寫

1. Let me explain the ▆▆▆ of reading preferences to you.

2. This is the ▆▆▆ contract our company signs with designers.

3. You can ▆▆▆ me whenever you have questions about the insurance policy.

4. I can ▆▆▆ you another interior design if this one does not please you.

空格

1. chart

2. standard

3. contact

4. show

翻譯

1. 讓我來為你解讀這張閱讀偏好。

2. 這是我們公司用來跟客戶簽的指示合約。

3. 如果您有任何關於保險條約的問題，請跟我聯絡。

4. 如果這個您不喜歡的話，我可以提供另一個室內設計照片給您看。

track 046

(2) 跟讀

We appreciate you for bringing the laptop with you to show us.
我們感謝您帶筆電來展示給我們看。

If you take a close look at the model, you can notice the adjustment the designers made.
如果你仔細看這個模特兒，你會發現設計師所做的修改。

As you know, the sales performance of last year is to be improved.
如你所知道的，銷售業績有待改善。

As you probably noticed, the sales figures of e-books sales broke the record.
可能你也發現了，電子書的銷售量破紀錄。

(3) 在電腦前討論注意事項

描述在電腦前討論常會出現的字彙&片語：

agreement (n.)	同意
arbitrator (n.)	仲裁
chart(n.)	圖表
contract (n.)	合約
decrease (n. v.)	減少
figure (n.)	數目
growth (n.)	成長
negotiation (n.)	協商

九、一男一女正在餐廳面對面吃晚餐

例題：

◆ **Look at the picture on your test book.**

(A) They are cooking the meal together.

(B) They are complaining about the food.

(C) They are studying the menu together.

(D) They are enjoying their meal together.

中文翻譯：

◆ 看試題冊上的這張照片。

(A) 他們正在一起烹飪。

(B) 他們正在抱怨餐點。

(C) 他們正在一起研究菜單。

(D) 他們正在一起享用餐點。

正確選項：D

(1) 聽寫

1. The wine ▓▓▓▓ quite special to me.

2. It is nice to be together after all ▓▓▓▓ years.

3. I haven't had a ▓▓▓▓ light dinner for a long time.

4. When did you decide to be a ▓▓▓▓ ?

空格

1. tastes

2. these

3. candle

4. vegan

翻譯

1. 這酒嚐起來挺特別的。

2. 多年不見再相逢，真是不錯。

3. 我好久沒有吃頓燭光晚餐了。

4. 你何時決定成為純素者？

track 047

(2) 跟讀

How do you like your choice of food?
你點的餐點好吃嗎？

Thank you so much for accepting my dinner invitation.
謝謝您接受了我的晚餐邀請。

If you want to, we can order desserts, such as carrot cake with ice cream.
如果你喜歡的話，我們可以點甜點，例如紅蘿蔔蛋糕配冰淇淋。

Thank you for spending some time around Christmas with me.
謝謝你在聖誕節時還花時間陪我。

(3) 晚餐注意事項

描述共進晚餐常會出現的字彙&片語：

appetizer (n.)	開胃菜
candle light dinner (n.)	燭光晚餐
feast (n.)	饗宴
main course (n.)	主菜
portion (n.)	份量
salad (n.)	沙拉
toast (n. v.)	敬酒
turkey (n.)	火雞
wine (n.)	酒

十、一個男子正在辦公室整理資料夾

例題：

◆ **Look at the picture on your test book.**

(A) The folders are database of customers.

(B) The man lost a folder somewhere.

(C) The secretary is compiling the documents.

(D) The man filing the folders in the office.

中文翻譯：

◆ 看試題冊上的這張照片。

(A) 這些檔案夾是客戶的資料庫。

(B) 這男子在這裡遺失了一個資料夾。

(C) 這秘書正在整理資料。

(D) 這男子正在辦公室整理資料夾。

正確選項：D

(1) 聽寫

1. The boss ▇▇▇ on his secretary to find the infor mation in the folders.

2. Nowadays you can find almost anything online; therefore, there is no need to keep everything in ▇▇ ▇▇ .

3. Our ▇▇▇ Manager keeps a folder for the personal data of every employee in this company.

4. Some people have ▇▇▇ about putting files in the cloud.

空格

1. relies
2. folders
3. Human Resources
4. reservation

翻譯

1. 老闆靠秘書才能找到資料夾中的資料。
2. 現在網路上幾乎應有盡有，因此沒有必要將所有資料建檔。
3. 我們人資經理將公司用資料夾將所有員工的個資建檔。
4. 有的人對於將檔案放於雲端有所顧忌。

(2) 跟讀

Some people print out all documents and put them into a folder.
有些人列印出所有文件，然後放入資料夾中。

It is easy to access folders in an archive room.
在檔案室中找資料夾很容易。

Young professionals prefer storing all files and charts in the cloud.
年輕的專業人士偏愛將檔案與照片表存在雲端。

Security is essential in storing company data.
安全對保存公司數據非常重要。

(3) 整理資料夾注意事項

描述整理資料夾常會出現的字彙&片語：

confidential (adj.)	機密的
file the folders (phr.)	整理資料夾
in alphabetic order (phr.)	依照字母順序
in chronological order (phr.)	依照時間順序
secure (adj.)	安全的
SOP = standard operation procedure (n.)	標準作業程序
sort out (phr.)	整理

track 049

十一、 一個女子拿著一張提款卡站在自動提款機前

例題：

◆ **Look at the picture on your test book.**

(A) The young woman is holding a card before an ATM.

(B) The young woman does not have money in her bank account.

(C) The young woman is going to remit some money.

(D) The young woman has never used an ATM before.

中文翻譯：

◆ 看試題冊上的這張照片。

(A) 這小姐正拿著提款卡站在自動提款機前。

(B) 這小姐的帳戶裡沒有錢。

(C) 這小姐正要轉帳。

(D) 這小姐從來沒有用過自動提款機。

正確選項：A

(1) 聽寫

1. How often do you ▦▦ cash with an ATM?

2. Be aware of ▦▦ people when you are operating an ATM.

3. You can see your ▦▦ history in your passbook.

4. On the top of this ATM there is often a passbook ▦▦ machine.

空格

1. withdraw

2. suspicious

3. transaction

4. update

翻譯

1. 你多久於自動提款機提一次款？

2. 操作自動提款機時要提防可以人士。

3. 你可以於存摺裡看見交易紀錄。

4. 這台自動提款機上部有一個補摺機。

track 050

(2) 跟讀

Most people withdraw cash with an ATM.
大部分人用自動提款機來提款。

You can check your account balance with an ATM.
你可以用自動提款機來查存款餘額。

Some people remit money from one account to another with an ATM.
有些人用自動提款機來轉帳。

The interest rate of borrowing money with an ATM with a credit card is too high.
用信用卡於自動提款機借錢，利息太高。

(3) 自動提款機前事項

描述在自動提款機前常會出現的字彙&片語：

ATM = automated teller machine (n.)
　　　　　　　　　　　　自動提款機
deposit (v.)　　　　　　　存款
passbook = bankbook (n.)　存摺
PIN number (PIN = Personal Identification Number)
　　　　　　　　　　　　密碼，個人身分識別碼
remit (v.)　　　　　　　　匯款
remittance (n.)　　　　　　匯款
savings account (n.)　　　儲蓄存款戶頭
transfer (n. v.)　　　　　轉帳
withdraw (v.)　　　　　　提款
withdrawal (n.)　　　　　提款

track 051

十二、一群年輕員工正在聽一位主管的指示

例題：

◆ **Look at the picture on your test book.**

(A) They seem to dislike the group discussion.

(B) They seem to have a good team spirit in discussion.

(C) They seem to disregard the supervisor's opinions.

(D) They seem to be strangers to each other.

中文翻譯：

◆ 看試題冊上的這張照片。

(A) 他們似乎不喜歡團體討論。

(B) 他們似乎帶著團隊精神在討論。

track 051

(C) 他們似乎不管主管的意見。

(D) 他們似乎對彼此很陌生。

正確選項：B

(1) 聽寫

1. The supervisor and his staff members are talking about issues about their _____.

2. The topic of their discussion is _____ customer service.

3. Many cases of customer _____ are raised during the brainstorm.

4. The manager asks them to put more _____ into their work.

空格

1. clients

2. regarding

3. complaints

4. effort

翻譯

1. 一位主管與他的員工正在討論客戶問題。

2. 他們討論的主題關於客戶服務。

3. 在腦力激盪時，很多客戶抱怨的個案被提出來討論。

4. 經理要求他們更加努力工作。

(2) 跟讀

They are giving their feedback to the senior supervisor.
他們提供資深主管意見回饋。

They listen attentively to the speaking supervisor.
他們專注地聆聽主管說話。

The weekly meeting on every Monday morning is energizing to staff members.
每星期一的週會對員工來說很能提振士氣。

They report to the supervisor their work progress during the small group meeting.
他們在小組會議時向主管報告工作進度。

(3) 主管與下屬討論事項

描述主管與下屬討論時常會出現的字彙&片語：

brainstorm (v.)	腦力激盪
client (n.)	客戶
customer complaint (n.)	客訴
customer service (n.)	客戶服務
debate (n. v.)	辯論
discussion (n.)	討論
feedback (n.)	回饋
instruction (n.)	教導
teamwork (n.)	團隊合作

track 052

模擬試題 6 題

1. **Look at the picture marked number one on your test book.**

   (A) A man is jogging.

   (B) A man is asking for help.

   (C) A man is running away from fire.

   (D) A man is looking for his missing dog.

中文翻譯：

1. 看試題冊上第 1 題的這張照片。

   (A) 一個男子正在慢跑。

   (B) 一個男子正在求救。

   (C) 一個男子正在逃離火場。

   (D) 一個男子正在尋找走丟的狗。

track 053

正確選項：A

2. Look at the picture marked number two on your test book.

(A) There are many readers in this library.

(B) The bookshelves are filled with books.

(C) The librarians are sorting out the books.

(D) The library has many computers.

中文翻譯：

2. 看試題冊上第 **2** 題的這張照片。

(A) 在照片書館裡有很多讀者。

(B) 書架上有很多書籍。

(C) 照片書館員正在整理書籍。

(D) 照片書館有很多電腦。

track 053

正確選項：B

3. **Look at the picture marked number three on your test book.**

(A) The young woman is cleaning the desks.

(B) The young woman is making some coffee.

(C) The young woman is talking to herself.

(D) The young woman is using a copy machine.

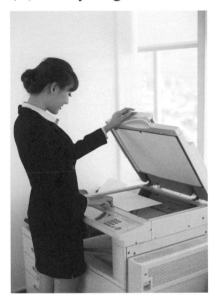

中文翻譯：

3. 看試題冊上第 **3** 題的這張照片。

(A) 這位小姐正在清理桌子。

(B) 這位小姐正在煮咖啡。

(C) 這位小姐正在跟自己說話。

(D) 這位小姐正在使用影印機。

正確選項：D

4. Look at the picture marked number four on your test book.

(A) This is a factory.

(B) They are printing machines.

(C) This is a laundromat.

(D) This is a convenience store.

中文翻譯：

4. 看試題冊上第 4 題的這張照片。

   (A) 這是間工廠。

   (B) 這些是印刷機器。

   (C) 這是間自助洗衣店。

   (D) 這是間便利商店。

正確選項：C

track 054

5. Look at the picture marked number five on your test book.

(A) A man is walking under an umbrella.

(B) There are many cars on the road.

(C) There is no rain at all now.

(D) There is a typhoon here.

中文翻譯：

5. 看試題冊上第 5 題的這張照片。

(A) 一男子正稱著傘走路。

(B) 路上有很多車。

(C) 現在一點也沒有雨。

(D) 這裡有颱風。

正確選項：A

 track 055

6. Look at the picture marked number six on your test book.

(A) There is a toll station.

(B) There is a car accident.

(C) There are many cars on the highway.

(D) There are many police officers here.

中文翻譯：

6. 看試題冊上第 6 題的這張照片。

　(A) 這裡有個收費站。

　(B) 這裡有個車禍。

　(C) 高速公路上很多車子。

　(D) 這裡有很多警察。

正確選項：C

track 055

Part

2 應答問題

Directions : You will hear a question or statement and three responses spoken in English. They will not be printed in your test book and will be spoken only one time. Select the best response to the question or statement and mark the letter (A), (B), or (C) on your answer sheet.

解說：你會聽到一個用英語表達的問題或陳述，還有三個回答，這些都不會印在測驗本上，而且只播放一次，請選出對於此問題或陳述的最佳反應，然後在答案紙上劃記(A)或 (B)或 (C)。

範例

7. Mark your answer on your answer sheet.

請作答

A：Where is the new fax machine?

B：

(A) Next to the water fountain.

(B) I'll send a fax tomorrow.

(C) By Wednesday.

A：新的傳真機在哪裡呢？

B：

(A) 飲水機的旁邊。

(B) 明天我會傳真過去。

(C) 星期三前。

正確選項：(A)

解析：

從此問題的第一個字 Where 知道是要問位置地方，答案選項中只有 (A)適合。

---

1. 注意重點

於這個項目中，必須聆聽播放出來的題目內容，接著從播放出來的 3 個答案選項中，挑選出最適合的回答。問題與答案選項都不會印於試題冊上，所以必須要仔細聆聽。

生活化片語最近經常成為測驗重點，如果沒有聽過，可以就上下文來猜測，例如：get out 少來了； shut up 別鬧了。

---

2. 出題類型

(1) 以疑問詞開始的問句（5 W 1 H）

這一類是以疑問詞 5 W 1 H （who, what, when, where, why, how）開始為問句來發問，答案通常非常固定，不會有Yes 或No 出現，因此只要聽清楚疑問詞、主詞＆動詞，通常會很容易找到正確答案的。

track 056

範例：

(W-Am): How did you like the movie?

(M-Br): (A) Never mind.

(B) It is a good movie.

(C) It will do.

正確答案：(B)

（女－美）：你喜歡這部電影嗎？

（男－英）：(A)沒關係。

(B)是好電影。

(C)這樣可以。

(2) Yes / No 問句

含助動詞或間接問句的肯定疑問句，通常以Yes / No 來回答，所以常稱為 Yes / No 問句，如果不是以Yes / No 回答，那麼就要看句意來選擇能和問題搭配起來自然流暢的選項，例如：I think so, I don't know, Not that I heard of, It hasn't been decided yet 等等。

範例：

(W-Cn): Did you choose one of the candidates?

(M-Aus): (A) Yes, he chose the project.

(B) No, none of them.

(C) I have no choice.

track 057

正確答案：(B)

（女：加）：你選了這些求職者當中的一位嗎？

（男：澳）：(A)是的，他選了這個企劃案。

　　　　　　(B)沒有，都沒入選。

　　　　　　(C)我沒有其它選擇。

(3) 選擇型問句

選擇A 或B的題目，通常答案有 3 種：

A 或B其中之一

都可以：Either is fine with me.

都不好：I like neither of them.

範例：

(M-Br):　Are you looking for a full-time or a part-time position?

(W-Am): (A) I'll do my best.

　　　　 (B) It takes time.

　　　　 (C) I prefer working half day.

正確答案：(C)

（男－英）：你正在找全職還是兼差的工作？

（女－美）：(A)我會盡我所能。

　　　　　　(B)需要花時間。

　　　　　　(C)我比較喜歡工作半天。

track 057

(4) 附加問句

只需要將有附加問句的句子當成一般的肯定句或否定句來處理即可，答案可以Yes / No 回答也可以不用Yes / No。

範例：

(M-Br):　You like the French cuisine, don't you?

(W-Cn):　(A) No, it isn't.

　　　　　(B) Yes, very much.

　　　　　(C) No, nobody.

正確答案：(B)

（男－英）：妳喜歡法國料理，對吧？

（女－加）：(A)不，不是的。

　　　　　　(B)是的，非常喜歡。

　　　　　　(C)沒有，沒人。

(5) 否定問句

注意回答方式（Yes 肯定 / No 否定）

不論是以肯定或否定的疑問句來問，只要答案是肯定的，都要用Yes 來回答；反之，只要答案是否定的，都要用No 來回答。

 track 058

範例：

(M-Am): Isn't that the work schedule you are holding?

(W-Br): (A) Yes, our manager just gave it to me.

　　　　(B) No, we've run out of time.

　　　　(C) Let's time your work.

正確答案：(A)

（男－美）：妳手上拿的不是工作進度表嗎？

（女－英）：(A)是的，我們經理剛給我的。

　　　　　　(B)不是的，我們沒時間了。

　　　　　　(C)我們來量一下你工作的時間。

(6) 邀請，含祈使句

Why don't you/we…?　你何不／我們何不……？

What about…?　要不要……？

How about…?　要不要……？

Would you like…?　你想不想……？

Let's…　讓我們來……？

Why don't you…? 通常不同於以 Why 開頭的問句，所以不要選用 ” Because ” 開頭的選項。

常見的回答有：

Sounds good.　聽來不錯。

That's a good idea.　那是個好主意。

Thank you for your advice.　謝謝你的建議。

Let's go.　我們走吧。

其它能配合句意的選項，例如例題：

範例：

(M-Am): Let's go to the workshop!

(W-Br):　(A) How did it go?

　　　　　(B) How come?

　　　　　(C) What is it about?

正確答案：(C)

（男－美）：我們一起去工作坊吧！

（女－英）：(A)進行得怎麼樣？

　　　　　　(B)為什麼？

　　　　　　(C)是什麼樣的工作坊呢？

(7) 陳述意見的肯定句或否定句

　　陳述句，考的是互動，只要是能夠讓兩者的對話流暢自然的回答，都可能是正確選項。

　　在作答時挑選答案的難度對考生而言偏高，因為比較難以預料答話。

 track 059

通常如果以陳述句發問，常會以陳述句回答，不限肯定或否定句。

答案通常不會是以 Yes 或 No 開始的句子，雖然也會有例外但機率不高。

範例：

(W-Br): The new tea of that health food store is on sale.

(M-Am): (A) Who is selling tea?

(B) I will check it out.

(C) The food is nutritious.

正確答案：(B)

（女－英）：那家健康食品店的新到茶葉在特價。

（男－美）： (A)誰在賣茶葉？

(B)讓我來看看。

(C)食品很有營養。

綜合以上，聽力Part 2 常考的問句類型總整理：

分類	問句類型	例句
(1)	**Wh-** 問句	**Who/ What/ When/ Where/ Why/ Which/ How** 用上面的疑問詞開始的問句 例句： **Where are you?**
(2)	**Yes / No** 問句 含助動詞 （表提議） **Do, Be, Have, Can/Will/Should** 疑問句	**Do you like dancing?** **Would you like dancing with me?** **Could you do me a favor?** **May I speak to Mr. Lee?**
		含間接問句 例句： **Do you know when she will be back?**
(3)	選擇型問句	**Do you want steak or chicken?**
(4)	附加問句	**You like English, don't you?** **You don't like English, do you?**
(5)	否定問句	**Don't you like English?**
(6)	祈使句 建議和請求疑問句	**Let's watch TV.** **How about watching TV?**
(7)	陳述意見的肯定句 或否定句 重點提示： 直述句 考的是：互動	**That English test is hard.** **That English test isn't hard.**

track 060

3. 應對策略

(1)Wh-疑問句，不能用Yes/No來回答

(2) 小心容易混淆的回答

發音完全相同或相似的選項，常常是陷阱，不會是正確答案。

(3) 注意重覆出現的單字，通常是陷阱

同義字，例如：change 改變vs.零錢

(4) 注意間接回答

只要能使語意通順的答案都是正確答案。

1. 不知道

I don't know. 我不知道。

I have no idea. 我不曉得。

I am not sure. 我不確定。

I don't know what is happening 我不知道發生了什麼事。

I don't know what is going on. 我不知道怎麼一回事。

I am not in the loop. 我不清楚。

2. 還沒決定

It hasn't been decided yet. 還沒有定案。

There are no updates. 沒有新消息。

It's up in the air. 還沒有決定。

track 060

3. 還沒聽過

Not that I am aware of.　我不知情。

Not that I know of.　我不知道。

I haven't been informed of it.　我沒聽說。

I haven't heard of it.　我沒聽過。

4. 都可以，無所謂

It's up to you.　看你而定。

You can decide on it.　你可以做決定。

It doesn't matter.　都沒關係。

I am alright with whatever you choose.　你決定什麼都可以。

5. 要看誰／什麼狀況而定

It depends all on the client.　這一切要看客戶而定。

It depends on the weather.　要看天氣而定。

We'll have to see.　我們再看看吧。

It's up to our luck.　要看我們的運氣。

Let the future take care of it.　順其自然吧。

6. 我會去問一下或確認一下

Let me find it out.　我去查一下。

I'll check it and let you know.　我來查一下再告訴你。

I'll ask around.　我再問一下。

I'll google it and tell you the result.　我用古歌搜尋一下再告訴你結果。

Why don't you look it up?　你為什麼不查一下？

 track 061

Part 3 簡短對話

Directions: You will hear some conversations between two or more people. You will be asked to answer three questions about what the speakers say in each conversation. Select the best response to each question and mark the letter (A), (B), (C), or (D) on your answer sheet. The conversations will not be printed in your test book and will be spoken only one time.

解說：你會聽到兩人或多人之間的對話，你必須要回答關於每段對話的三個問題，請選出每個問題的最佳答案，然後在答案紙上劃記(A)或 (B)或 (C)或 (D)，這些對話不會在你的測驗本上印出來，而且只會播放一次。

範例

32. Why is the woman calling?

  (A) To cancel an order.

  (B) To complain about a product.

  (C) To redeem a gift card.

  (D) To renew a warranty.

32. 這位女子為什麼打電話？

  (A) 為了取消訂單。

track 061

(B) 為了抱怨一個產品。

(C) 為了兌換一張禮卷。

(D) 為了更新一個保固。

33. What does the man ask the woman about?

(A) A model name.

(B) A brand of coffee.

(C) A catalog number.

(D) A date of purchase.

33. 這個男子問女子關於什麼的問題？

(A) 一個產品型號。

(B) 一個咖啡品牌。

(C) 一個型錄號碼。

(D) 一個購買日期。

34. What does the man offer to do?

(A) Provide a discount.

(B) Send a free sample.

(C) Extend a warranty.

(D) Issue a refund.

34. 這個男子提供了什麼？

(A) 提供特價。

(B) 送免費樣品。

(C) 延長保固期。

(D) 提供換貨。

 track 062

正確選項：32 (B)；33. (D)；34. (A)

對話中譯

A：Hello, I'm calling about a coffee machine I purchased from your website. It's stopped working even though I haven't had it for very long. I expected it to last much longer than this.

B：Oh, I'm sorry to hear that. Our warranty covers products for up to a year. Do you know when you bought it?

A：I've had it for a little more than a year, so the warranty is probably just expired. This is so disappointing.

B：Well, I'll tell you what we can do. Although we can't replace it, since you are a valued customer, we can offer you a coupon for 40% off for your next purchase.

A：您好，我是為了在你們網站上買的咖啡機而打電話來，我才剛買不久就故障了，我還以為可以耐用得多。

B：不好意思會這樣，我們產品有一年的保固期，您知道何時購買的嗎？

A：我買了有一年多一點，所以剛好過了保固期，真是令人失望。

B：這樣子吧，雖然我們不能換新的給您，但因為您是貴賓級顧客，我們可以提供您六折的禮券供下次使用。

1. 注意重點

　　對話還沒播放前，要先快速略讀 3 個試題的題目與選項，若無時間，至少要掃讀題目與選項的關鍵字，預先做好心理準備。

　　作答完一題，要快速略讀下題的題目與選項，以此步驟進行下去，快速完成 3 個試題後，必須有時間於下組對話還沒播放前，先快速略讀 3 個試題的題目與選項，保持這個速度與節奏作答下去。

　　題目通常是按照文章內容先後順序來發問。

常見的題目特徵：

(1) 第一個題目的特徵：

　　通常與主題相關。

　　絕對要注意聽對話的開場白，好掌握內容大意。

　　例如：

例 What is the main idea?
　　大意是什麼？

例 What is this discussion mainly about?
　　這段討論主要關於什麼？

例 What is the general topic of this conversation?
　　這段會話的主題是什麼？

(2) 第二個題目的特徵：

　　通常與細節（5W1H）相關，關鍵在於先閱讀題目&選項，記住關鍵字，播放對話時才能專心聆聽與關鍵字相關部分。

(3) 第三個題目的特徵：

通常在測驗最後一位說話者所說內容，或是兩位說話者最後討論的相關事項，所以要注意聆聽這些部分，特別常會考的是 " 將來 " 會發生的事情或採取的行動。

例如：

例 What will the man do after this talk?
這個男子在這段談話後會做什麼？

例 What have they decided to do after this discussion?
他們決定在這段討論後做什麼？

(4) 改制後新多益加入2 組三人對話，加入 1 組圖表，例如價目表、火車時刻表、通訊軟體對話等等。

(5) 改制後新多益測驗生活化片語，例如：get out少來了， shut up別鬧了。

2. 出題類型

主題與目的	Topic
內容事物細節	**What**
內容人物細節	**Who**
內容地點細節	**Where**
內容時間細節	**When**
內容原因細節	**Why**
內容方式細節	**How**

3. 常見場景

Unit 1 出差情境

Unit 2 辦公室新面孔

Unit 3 請假事項

Unit 4 簡報

Unit 5 討論價格(3人)

Unit 6 參加商展(3人)

Unit 7 商務電話

Unit 8 通訊軟體

Unit 9 視訊會議(3人)

Unit 10 排除故障

Unit 11 臨時派遣工

Unit 12 升遷

Unit 13 茶水間閒聊

以下就各Unit一一列舉情境對話、新多益範例、常見單字與片語：

符號註解：

Am＝美國

Cn＝加拿大

Br＝英國

Aus＝澳洲

 track 064

Unit 1 出差情境

1. 情境對話

常見對話

Ⓐ I am sorry to tell you that all seats of Taiwan High Speed Rail to Kaohsiung are booked up.
很抱歉，所有高鐵到高雄的座位都被訂光了。

Ⓑ Is there any other way you can help us?
您還有其他什麼辦法嗎？

Ⓐ If you don't mind taking the regular train, there are seats available. It would take about 4.5 to 6 hours.
如果您不介意搭普通車，有空座位可訂，需要 4.5 到6 小時。

Ⓑ In that case, I will postpone the trip and reserve HSR next time in advance.
既然如此，我想要延期出遊，下次會提早訂高鐵。

換句話說

Ⓐ I am afraid that there is no seat available to Kaohsiung on Taiwan High Speed Rail.
很抱歉，高鐵到高雄的座位都被訂光了。

track 064

B How about other connections?

是否有其他交通方式？

A If the regular train is all right with you, we can book seats there for you. The trip takes around 4.5 to 6 hours.

如果您願意搭普通車，我們可以為您訂位，需要 4.5 到 6 小時。

B If so, I will reserve seats on HSR early next time.

如果是這樣的話，我下次再早點訂高鐵好了。

2. 新多益範例

(M-Am): Could you tell me if there is a decent hotel near this train station?

(W-Br): There are quite a few hotels in this area, and the quality depends on what price range you are thinking about.

(M-Am): That's great. Since my company pays for this business trip, I think I'll choose a high-end hotel with a gym this time.

(W-Br): In that case, Sheraton Grand Taipei Hotel might be a good choice. It's two blocks from here. If you keep walking straight, you won't miss it.

track 065

（女－英）：請問火車站這附近哪裡有不錯的飯店？

（男－美）：這地方有好幾家飯店，品質依照你想出的價錢而定。

（女－英）：太好了，既然我公司會支付這次出差費用，我想這次我會選擇一家高檔有健身中心的飯店。

（男－美）：既然如此，台北喜來登大飯店或許是很好的選擇，距離這裡兩個街口，如果你直走下去就一定會看見的。

(1) What are they mainly discussing?

(A) Traffic condition.

(B) Accommodation.

(C) Train station.

(D) Travel.

(1) 他們主要在討論什麼？

(A) 交通。

(B) 住宿。

(C) 火車站。

(D) 旅遊。

正確答案：B

(2) What did the man ask the woman to suggest?

(A) A local pub.

(B) A youth hostel.

track 065

(C) A Bed & Breakfast.

(D) An expensive hotel.

(2) 男子要求女子建議什麼？

(A) 當地酒吧。

(B) 青年旅館。

(C) 民宿。

(D) 昂貴的飯店。

正確答案：D

(3) What is the purpose for the man to come to this area?

(A) Leisure.

(B) Visiting relatives.

(C) For work.

(D) For studies.

(3) 男子到這地方的目的為何？

(A) 度假。

(B) 拜訪親戚。

(C) 為了工作。

(D) 為了學業。

正確答案：C

 track 066

3. 常見單字與片語

常見單字	片語
accommodation (n.) 住宿 [əˈkɑməˈdeʃən]	**arrange accommodation** 安排住宿
agency (n.) 代辦處 [ˈedʒənsɪ]	**a travel agency** 旅行社
book (v.) 預訂 [bʊk]	**book a flight** 訂機票
confirm(v.) 確認 [kənˈfɝm]	**confirm the reservation** 確認訂位
flight (n.) 航班 [flaɪt]	**an international flight** 國際航班
hospitality (n.) 殷勤好客，招待 [ˌhɑspɪˈtælətɪ]	**the hospitality of this hotel** 這家旅館的殷勤好客
itinerary (n.) 旅遊行程表 [aɪˈtɪnəˈrɛrɪ]	**prepare the itinerary** 準備旅遊行程表
reserve (v.) 預定 [rɪˈzɝv]	**reserve a hotel room** 預定旅館房間
return ticket (phr.) 回程機票 [rɪˈtɝn ˈtɪkɪt]	**purchase a return ticket** 購買回程機票
round-trip ticket (phr.) 來回機票 [ˈraʊndtrɪp ˈtɪkɪt]	**book a round-trip ticket** 預定來回機票

Unit 2 辦公室新面孔

1. 情境對話

常見對話

A You must be the new sales assistant, Ms. Lu.
妳一定是新來的業務助理陸小姐。

B Yes, you can all me Lily.
是的,您可以叫我莉莉。

A I heard you have worked in New York.
我聽說妳曾在紐約工作過。

B That was on an internship for 6 months with no pay.
那是 6 個月的無薪實習。

換句話說

A If I am correct, you are Ms. Lu, the new sales assistant.
如果我沒記錯,妳是陸小姐,新業務助理。

B That's right. Please just call me Lily.
沒錯,請叫我莉莉。

A They say you had a job in Big Apple previously.
聽說之前妳在紐約工作。

B It was an intern job with no salary for half a year.
那是半年無支薪的實習工作。

 track 067

2. 新多益範例

(M-Cn): Have you met our new sales manager, Todd Richardson? He just arrived in Taiwan from Hong Kong last night, and will be in the office next Monday.

(W-Aus): No, I haven't, but I have heard many good things about him. He held quite a few successful sales events while he was at our branch office in Hong Kong.

(M-Cn): Could you please show him around our office building and the factory nearby? I was going to do it myself, but something came up suddenly.

(W-Aus): Sure, no problem. It's my pleasure, and I can get to know more about him.

(M-Cn): Thank you so much. You are always so helpful.

（男－加）：妳見過我們的新業務經理陶德理查森嗎？他昨晚剛從香港來到台灣，下星期一會進辦公室。

（女－澳）：還沒有見過，不過我聽說過很多他的好評，他在我們香港分公司舉辦了不少場成功的銷售大會。

（男－加）：可以請妳到處帶他參觀我們辦公室還有周圍的工廠嗎？我本來要自己來，但是突然有事情要忙。

（女－澳）：當然可以，沒問題，這是我的榮幸，而且我可以更加認識他。

（男－加）：非常謝謝妳，妳總是如此樂於助人。

(1) What is the topic of their conversation?

(A) The new intern.

(B) The new manager.

(C) The new office.

(D) The new position.

(1) 他們對話的主題是什麼？

(A) 新實習生。

(B) 新經理。

(C) 新辦公室。

(D) 新職位。

正確答案：B

(2) Where did Mr. Richardson work before?

(A) Taiwan.

(B) Tokyo.

(C) Singapore.

(D) Hong Kong.

track 068

(2) 理查森之前在哪裡工作？

(A) 台灣。

(B) 東京。

(C) 新加坡。

(D) 香港。

正確答案：D

(3) What is the woman going to do for the man?

(A) Taking Mr. Richardson to welcome dinner.

(B) Helping Mr. Richard find accommodation.

(C) Giving Mr. Richardson a tour of the work environment.

(D) Holding a press conference for Mr. Richardson.

(3) 這位女子會為男子做什麼？

(A) 帶理查森先生去參加歡迎晚餐會。

(B) 幫助理查森先生找住宿地方。

(C) 帶理查森先生參觀工作環境。

(D) 為理查森先生舉行記者會。

正確答案：C

track 068

3. 常見單字與片語

常見單字	片語
allocation (n.) 分配 [ˈælə`keʃən]	**resource allocation** 資源分配
asset (n.) 資產 [`æsɛt]	**an asset to the company** 公司的資產
background (n.) 背景 [`bækˈgraʊnd]	**background investigation** 背景調查
colleague (n.) 同事 [kɑ`lig]	**colleagues in the same department** 同部門的同事
coworker (n.) 同事 [`koˈwɝkɚ]	**complaints about coworkers** 對同事的抱怨
expectation (n.) 期待 [ˈɛkspɛk`teʃən]	**meet the supervisor's expectation** 達到經理的期待
intern (n.) 實習生 [ɪn`tɝn]	**intern in a tech company** 科技公司的實習生
newcomer (n.) 新員工 [`njuˈkʌmɚ]	**a newcomer to the team** 團隊的新成員
orientation (n.) 職前訓練 [ˈorɪɛn`teʃən]	**employee orientation** 員工職前訓練
probation (n.) 試用 [pro`beʃən]	**probation period** 試用期

Unit 3 請假事項

1. 情境對話

常見對話

Ⓐ I will take maternity leave for eight weeks starting from Sep 13.

我要請 8 個星期的產假，從 9 月 13 日開始。

Ⓑ Please take good care.

請多保重。

Ⓐ Thank you. During that time, if you have any questions, please contact my colleague, Susan.

謝謝你，在這段時間如果你有任何問題，請聯絡我的同事蘇珊。

Ⓑ At the moment, I don't see the need, but thank you though.

現在我看沒有這個必要，但是還是謝謝妳。

換句話說

Ⓐ From Sep 13, I will be away from work because I am having a baby.

從 9 月 13 日起，我不會進辦公室，因為我要生產。

B Take good rest during this break.

在這段時間內好好休息。

A Thanks for saying that. In the meantime, Susan will be taking care of you if you have any issues.

謝謝你這麼說，在這期間如果你有任何問題，蘇珊會幫你。

B So far, I don't think I would need her service; nevertheless, thank you so much.

到目前為止我還不需要她的服務，不過，非常謝謝妳。

2. 新多益範例

(M-Br): Hello, I have to take a sick leave for a week. Could you tell me how to apply for it?

(W-Am): May I ask what specific illness you have?

(M-Br): I'm going to undergo a minor surgery on my right wrist next Wednesday, and my doctor requires me to rest for a week after that.

track 069

(W-Am): I see. You will have to fill out the form and put it in with the relevant medical certificate.

(M-Br): Thank you very much.

（男－英）：哈囉，我必須要請病假一星期，妳能告訴我如何申請嗎？

（女－美）：可以告訴我你的確切病名嗎？

（男－英）：我將會於下星期三進行一個右手腕的小手術，我的醫師要求我要在手術後休息一星期。

（女－美）：我了解了，你必須要填好這個表格，並且附上相關的醫療證明。

（男－英）：非常謝謝妳。

 track 070

(1) Why did the man call the woman?

(A) To apply for a maternal leave.

(B) To apply for reimbursement.

(C) To apply for a business travel.

(D) To apply for a leave for a surgery.

(1) 為什麼男子打電話給女子？

(A) 為了申請育嬰假。

(B) 為了申請補助。

(C) 為了申請出差。

(D) 為了申請手術病假。

正確答案：D

· track 070

(2) How long does the doctor require the man to rest after the operation?

(A) 5 days.

(B) 6 days.

(C) 7 days.

(D) 8 days.

(2) 醫師要求男子手術後休息多久？

(A) 5 天。

(B) 6 天。

(C) 7 天。

(D) 8 天。

正確答案：C

(3) What is the man required to submit along with the form?

(A) Medical bills.

(B) Medical certificate.

(C) Prescriptions.

(D) Insurance.

(3) 除了表格，男子要附上什麼？

(A) 醫療費用。

(B) 醫療證明。

(C) 處方。

(D) 保險。

正確答案：B

 track 071

3. 常見單字與片語

常見單字	片語
apply(v.) 申請 [əˋplaɪ]	**apply for** 申請
certificate(n.) 證明 [səˋtɪfəkɪt]	**medical certificate** 醫療證明
insurance(n.) 保險 [ɪnˋʃʊrəns]	**health insurance** 健康檢查
leave(n.) 休假 [liv]	**sick leave** 病假
load(n.) 負擔 [lod]	**heavy teaching load** 教學負擔很重
maternity(n.) (adj.) 母親身分； 產婦的 [məˋtɝnətɪ]	**maternity leave** 產假
overload(n.) 過重的負擔 [ˊ ovɚˋlod]	**information overload** 訊 息爆炸
paternity(n.) (adj.) 父親身分；父 親的	**paternity leave** 父親假
substitute (adj.) 替代的 [ˋsʌbstəˊ tjut]	**substitute teacher** 代課老師
valid (adj.) 有效的；合法的 [ˋvælɪd]	**a valid contract** 具有法律效力的合同

Unit 4 簡報

1.情境對話

常見對話

Ⓐ Ladies and gentlemen, it is my pleasure to give you a presentation about the performance of our department last year.

各位女士先生，我很榮幸在這裡向您做我們部門成績的簡報。

Ⓑ Excuse me, the projector seems to be not working.

不好意思，投影片似乎運作有問題。

Ⓐ Dan, could you take a close look of the technical issues?

丹，你可不可以看看出了什麼技術問題？

Ⓑ All right. Now it is very easy to see the charts and pictures.

好了，現在圖表與圖片都可以看得很清楚。

換句話說

track 072

Ⓐ Good morning everyone, it is my honor to talk to you about what we have done in the past year.

各位早安，很榮幸可以在這裡跟您報告我們去年的成果。

track 072

B Wait a minute, something must go wrong with the projector.

等一下，一定是投影機出問題了。

A Will you please fix the technical problems, Dan?

丹，你可不可以處理一下技術問題？

B Okay now. The graphical aids are becoming very clear.

現在好了，輔助圖表現在變得很清楚了。

2. 新多益範例

(M-Am): Have you prepared the Power Point of the presentation yet? Our American Manager of the Asian Region is coming tomorrow morning.

(W-Br): It's not that hard for me because all I have to do is to change the previous data of the same formats from the Finance Department.

(M-Am): Lucky you. The manager asked me to give a small talk on how to becomea great salesperson. Although I have years of experiences in Sales Department, it's hard for me to put them into words.

track 072

(W-Br): Before giving the presentation, you can rehearse it in front of me first. I'll give you my honest opinion.

（男－美）：你們準備好了簡報的Power Point嗎？我們的美籍亞洲區經理明天早上要過來。

（女－英）：這對我來說不難，因為我只要將財務部門格式上的數據改變一下就可以了。

（男－美）：妳真好運。經理要求我講一下如何成為一位優秀業務員，雖然我有多年的業務部門工作經驗，要我用話語來描述，很難。

（女－英）：你可以在簡報前跟我演練一遍，我會給你忠實的意見。

(1) What most likely are the relationship of the two speakers?

    (A) Classmates.

    (B) Colleagues.

    (C) Business partners.

    (D) Relatives.

(1) 這兩位說話者最可能是什麼關係？

    (A) 同學。

    (B) 同事。

    (C) 事業夥伴。

    (D) 親戚。

正確答案：B

track 073

(2) Why is it very easy for the woman to give the presentation?

(A) She has a lot of experiences.

(B) She remembers all data.

(C) She uses quite a few formats.

(D) She only has to fill in new data.

(2) 為什麼對女子來說，做簡報很容易？

(A) 她經驗豐富。

(B) 她記得很多數據。

(C) 她使用很多格式。

(D) 她只需要填入數據。

正確答案：D

(3) What does the woman suggest the man to do before giving thepresentation?

(A) To practice it before her.

(B) To show the data to her.

(C) To change the data for her.

(D) To sum up his experiences.

(3) 女子建議男子於簡報前做什麼？

(A) 在她面前練習。

(B) 展示數據給她看。

(C) 幫她改變數據。

(D) 將他的經驗做總結。

正確答案：A

track 073

3. 常見單字與片語

常見單字	片語
audience(n.) 觀眾 [ˋɔdɪəns]	**target audience** 目標觀眾
chart(n.) 圖表 [tʃɑrt]	**trend chart** 趨勢圖
conclusion(n.) 結論 [kənˋkluʒən]	**reach a conclusion** 達成結論
feedback(n.) 回饋 [ˋfidˏbæk]	**provide feedback** 提供回饋
figure(n.) 數字 [ˋfɪgjɚ]	**sales figures** 銷售數據
graph(n.) 圖表 [græf]	**line graph** 折線圖
material(n.) 資料 [məˋtɪrɪəl]	**course materials** 課程資料
presentation(n.) 簡報 [ˏprizɛnˋteʃən]	**make a presentation** 做簡報
projector(n.) 放映機；投影機 [prəˋdʒɛktɚ]	**equipped with a projector** 備有放映機
slide(n.) 幻燈片 [slaɪd]	**slides of art works** 藝術品的幻燈片

Unit 5 討論價格（3 人）

1. 情境對話

常見對話

A Christmas is coming soon. What about we send each of our clients a box of pineapple cake as a gift?

聖誕節快來了，我們要不要送每位客戶一盒鳳梨酥當禮物？

B It would be nice, but the postage fees would be quite high.

這個點子不錯，但是郵資會相當高。

A How much would that be roughly?

大概會多少錢呢？

B Take Japan for example, it would cost as much as the pineapple cake itself to send it by air mail.

就拿日本來說，寄鳳梨酥的空運郵資會跟鳳梨酥費用一樣貴。

換句話說

A It's again time for year-end gift shopping. What do you reckon if we give a box of pineapple cake to our clients?

track 074

又到了年底選購禮物時節了，你看我們送客戶一盒鳳梨酥怎麼樣？

B That sounds good, but it costs a fortune to deliver pineapple cake.
聽來不錯，但是運費很驚人。

A How much would it cost?
會需要多少費用呢？

B The delivery fee would be about the same as the pineapple cake.
運費會和鳳梨酥本身差不多。

2.新多益範例

	Price of a trip for delivering multiple meals (pre-paid) More than 5 people	Price of unlimited trips for delivering multiple meals for a month (pre-paid) More than 5 people
XSpeed	2.15 USD	35.99 USD
Black Bear	2.05 USD	33.99 USD
Flying Meal	1.99 USD	37.99 USD

track 075

Jeremy (M-Aus): Look, I just downloaded the price lists of meal delivery in this region. Let's decide which delivery company we should choose.

track 075

Jennifer (W-Br): Don't most delivery companies charge per trip, not per person?

Brad (M-Am): In that case, there is no need to decide yet because we can order it every morning.

Jeremy (M-Aus): Have you noticed they offer a special monthly price if we pay it in advance? With 9 people in our office, we can use the monthly group price.

Jennifer (W-Br): That's right. The Flying Meal company has the lowest price per trip, but the monthly fee is highest.

Brad (M-Am): I see. Now I can finally make sense of this comparative price table. It seems that the Black Bearcompany suits us best.

	送一趟的價格 一次可送多餐（預付） 5 人以上	以月計價的價格 不限趟數，一次可送多餐（預付） 5 人以上
Ｘ速	2.15 美金	35.99 美金
黑熊	2.05 美金	33.99 美金
飛餐	1.99 美金	37.99 美金

track 075

傑瑞米（男－澳）：你們看，我剛下載了此地區的外送價目表，讓我們來決定該選哪家外送公司。

珍妮佛（女－英）：大部分的外送公司不都是以趟計費，並非以人數計費的嗎？

布萊德（男－美）：既然如此，現在沒有決定的必要，我們可以每天早上再決定。

傑瑞米（男－澳）：你們是否注意到，如果我們預先付費，他們有提供特別月費？我們辦公室共有 9 人，我們可以使用團體月費。

珍妮佛（女－英）：對，飛行餐公司單趟價錢最低，但是月費最高。

布萊德（男－美）：我明白了，現在我總算看懂了這張價格比較表，看來黑熊公司最適合我們。

(1) What is the topic of their discussion?

(A) Preparing special diets.

(B) Sharing a car ride together.

(C) Getting bonus in the end of year.

(D) Paying for food delivered.

(1) 他們討論的主題是什麼？

(A) 準備特別食物。

(B) 一起搭車。

(C) 於年底分紅利。

(D) 餐點外送付費。

正確答案：D

track 075

(2) Why is it a good idea to pay monthly fee in advance?

(A) To get a special monthly price.

(B) To be able to choose a group menu.

(C) To have vouchers for next month.

(D) To avoid ordering meals every morning.

(2) 為什麼預先付費是個好主意？

(A) 能夠得到特別月費。

(B) 能夠選團體菜單。

(C) 能夠得到下個月的折價券。

(D) 能夠不必每早訂餐。

正確答案：A

track 076

(3) What is their reason for choosing the company?

(A) The fastest delivery.

(B) The best customer service.

(C) The lowest cost.

(D) The widest meal choices.

(3) 他們選擇這家公司的理由為何？

(A) 最快送達。

(B) 最佳客服。

(C) 最低價。

(D) 最多餐點選擇。

正確答案：C

track 076

3. 常見單字與片語

常見單字	片語
agreement(n.) 同意 [əˋgrimənt]	**reach an agreement** 達成協議
arrangement(n.) 安排 [əˋrendʒmənt]	**make arrangements** 做 安排
authorize(v.) 授權 [ˋɔθəˊraɪz]	**authorize payments** 授權付款
bargain (v.) 討價還價 [ˋbɑrgɪn]	**bargain for a lower price** 為了低一點的價格而議價
compromise (v.) 妥協 [ˋkɑmprəˊmaɪz]	**come to a compromise** 達成妥協
concession(n.) 退讓 [kənˋsɛʃən]	**make mutual concessions** 互相做了讓步
contract (n.) 合約 [kənˋtrækt]	**sign a contract** 簽訂合約
dispute (n.) (v.) 爭議 [dɪˋspjut]	**have a dispute** 起爭執
negotiation(n.) 協商 [nɪˊgoʃɪˋeʃən]	**enter into negotiation** 開始談判
priority(n.) 優先 [praɪˋɔrətɪ]	**a top priority** 最優先考慮的事

 track 077

Unit 6 參加商展（3 人）

1. 情境對話

常見對話

Ⓐ In less than one hour, this tea exhibition is going to end. We now offer buy one get one for free for all cans of tea.

再過不到一小時，這個茶葉展就要結束了，我們現在開始買一送一活動。

Ⓑ That's fantastic. I am interested in getting 7 cans of different green tea. Could I have half of the price for all tea?

太好了，我想要買7罐不同的綠茶，可以都算我半價嗎？

Ⓐ No problem. Do you need a gift bag for each can?

沒問題，您需要每罐一個袋子嗎？

Ⓑ As long as the bag is made of paper.

只要是紙袋就好。

換句話說

Ⓐ Soon the tea show is going to be closed. For all the tea here, you can get 2 cans while paying for only one.

茶葉展很快就結束了，這裡的茶都可以買一送一。

Ⓑ Sounds terrific. How about giving 50% off for all 7 cans I purchase?

聽來真不錯，如果我買7罐，可以都打五折嗎？

Ⓐ Sure. Would you like to have gift bags to go with the cans?

當然可以，您想要送禮用的袋子來裝罐子嗎？

Ⓑ Only if they are paper bags.

是紙製袋子就可以。

2. 新多益範例

David (M-Am): Welcome to the exhibition of Books of Children's Literature.

Amy (W-Aus): Thank you. I noticed that these books of yours could actually read stories out loud.

Ian (M-Br): Could you show us how it works?

David (M-Am): These books are like the reading platforms that can read e-books. All readers have to do is to press the bottom in front of each paragraph to listen to the reading.

Amy (W-Aus): Busy parents can then rely on them to read bedtime stories to their kids.

track 077

Ian (M-Br): Children can pick the stories they are interested in to listen to. That sounds great.

大衛（男－美）：歡迎來到兒童文學展。

艾美（女－澳）：謝謝，我注意到你們的書會大聲朗讀。

宜安（男－英）：可不可以示範一下如何操作？

大衛（男－美）：這些書就像是能夠朗讀電子書的閱讀平台，讀者只要按下每段文章前的按鈕來聽朗讀。

艾美（女－澳）：忙碌的父母可以靠這個來朗讀床邊故事給小孩聽。

宜安（男－英）：小孩可以挑他們感興趣的故事來聽，聽來真是太好了。

 track 078

(1) Where are the three speakers most likely to be at?

(A) A book fair.

(B) A Christmas market.

(C) A fashion runway.

(D) A car exhibition.

(1) 這三位說話者最可能身在何處？

(A) 書展。

(B) 聖誕市集。

(C) 時尚伸展台。

(D) 汽車展場。

track 078

正確答案：A

(2) Why would busy parents like the product?

(A) They prefer reading stories themselves.

(B) They can afford to buy the product.

(C) They do not like children's literature.

(D) They have little time to read to children.

(2) 為什麼忙碌的父母喜歡這個產品？

(A) 他們自身喜歡閱讀故事。

(B) 他們能夠買得起這個產品。

(C) 他們不喜歡兒童文學。

(D) 他們沒有時間為小孩朗讀。

正確答案：D

(3) What is NOT mentioned in their conversation?

(A) Similarity to E-books.

(B) Prices of the product.

(C) Target customers.

(D) Audio function.

(3) 他們對話中沒有提到什麼？

(A) 電子書的相似處。

(B) 這個產品的價錢。

(C) 目標客戶。

(D) 聽覺功能。

正確答案：B

3. 常見單字與片語

常見單字	片語
booth (n.) （有篷的）貨攤 [buθ]	**a refreshment booth** 餐飲攤
exhibition(n.) 展覽會 [ˌɛksəˋbɪʃən]	**an art exhibition** 藝術博覽會
exposition (n.) 博覽會 [ˌɛkspəˈzɪʃn]	**hold an international exposition** 舉行一次國際博覽會
fair(n.) 市集；展覽	**a book fair** 書展
flyer(n.) （廣告）傳單 [ˋflaɪɚ]	**hand out flyers** 發傳單
leaflet(n.) 傳單 [ˋliflɪt]	**distribute leaflet** 發傳單
show(n.) 展覽；展覽會 [ʃo]	**a fashion show** 時裝秀
stand(n.) 小攤 [stænd]	**a fruit stand** 水果攤
update (n.) (v.) 最新報導 [ˋʌpdet]	**provide a update** 提供最新報導
voucher (n.) 消費券 [ˋvaʊtʃɚ]	**a gift voucher** 禮券

Unit 7　商務電話

1. 情境對話

常見對話

Ⓐ Hello, this is Prince Dental Clinic. How can I help you?

您好，這裡是王子牙醫診所，需要什麼服務嗎？

Ⓑ I'd like to change the date of my reservation from Sep. 13 to Sep. 28.

我想要將我 9月13日的預約改成 9月28日。

Ⓐ Not a problem. Next time you can reschedule your appointment online if you want to.

沒問題，下次您可以在網路上更改預約。

Ⓑ Really? That can save me quite some time. Thank you.

真的嗎？那樣我可以節省不少時間，謝謝您。

換句話說

Ⓐ Prince Dental Clinic. What can I do for you?

王子牙醫診所，請問您需要什麼服務？

Ⓑ I have the appointment on Sep. 13, and I'd like to change it to Sep. 28 now.

我 9月13日有預約，現在想要改成 9月28日。

track 079

Ⓐ Sure. If it suits you, we have online reservation service
for you to reschedule your appointment.
當然沒問題，如果您方便的話，下次可以在網路預
約服務系統上更改預約。

Ⓑ I didn't know that. It would be much more efficient.
Thanks.
我還不知道呢，那樣會變得有效率多了，謝謝。

 track 080

2. 新多益範例

(W-Br): Hello, Sam, do you know this year our yearly
meeting will take place in Seoul instead of Tokyo?

(M-Am): Yes, I know it. Do you know why?

(W-Br): Some say that our CEO and CFO from the
UK would like to visit the newly-built factories in Korea
after the meeting.

(M-Am): I've never been to Seoul before, have you?

(W-Br): Me neither. Hopefully we can have some free
time to do a bit sightseeing together.

(M-Am): Thanks for calling me.

track 080

(女－英)：喂，山姆，你知道我們年度大會在漢城，而不是在東京舉行？

(男－美)：我知道，妳知道原因嗎？

(女－英)：有人說我們的英籍執行長和財務長想要於會議後參觀韓國新蓋的工廠。

(男－美)：我從來沒去過漢城，妳去過嗎？

(女－英)：我也沒有，希望我們會有些空閒時間一起觀光。

(男－美)：謝謝妳打電話過來。

(1) What is the main subject of this conversation?

(A) The destination for sightseeing this year.

(B) The new factory in a different city.

(C) The new CEO and CFO from the UK.

(D) The city of the annual meeting this year.

(1) 這場對話的主題為何？

(A) 年度觀光的目的地。

(B) 不同城市的新工廠。

(C) 英籍的執行長和財務長。

(D) 本年度會議的所在城市。

正確答案：D

track 081

(2) Why is the yearly meeting going to be held in Seoul?

(A) The managerial level is going to inspect a plant there.

(B) The employees can save travel budget for business trips.

(C) The new training courses will take place there.

(D) The project will involve many Koreans.

(2) 為什麼年度會議將於漢城舉行？

(A) 管理階層會檢查那裡的一座工廠。

(B) 員工將可省下出差的旅遊經費。

(C) 新的培訓課程會在那裡舉行。

(D) 這個專案會牽涉到很多韓國人。

正確答案：A

(3) What does the woman mean by "me neither"?

(A) She has never seen such a new factory before.

(B) She has never been to Seoul before.

(C) She cannot join the man to do sightseeing.

(D) She has not been on a business trip before.

(3) 這位女子説 **"me neither"** 是什麼意思？

(A) 她從來沒有見到這樣的新工廠。

(B) 她從來沒有到過漢城。

(C) 她不能跟男子一起觀光。

(D) 她從來沒出差過。

正確答案：B

track 081

3. 常見單字與片語

常見單字	片語
beep (n.) 嗶嗶的聲音 **[bip]**	**after the beep** 嗶聲後
connect (v.) 連接，連結 **[kəˋnɛkt]**	**connect with him** 與他接通電話
dial (v.) 撥號，打電話 **[ˋdaɪəl]**	**dial a wrong number** 打錯電話
directory (n.) 電話簿 **[dəˋrɛktərɪ]**	**a telephone directory** 電話簿
extension (n.) 電話分機 **[ɪkˋstɛnʃən]**	**an extension number** 分機號碼
message (n.) 訊息；消息 **[ˋmɛsɪdʒ]**	**leave amessage for her** 留話給她
reach (v.) 與……取得聯繫 **[ritʃ]**	**reach her** 聯繫到她
receive(v.) 收到 **[rɪˋsiv]**	**receive a phone call** 接到一通電話
record (n.) 紀錄 **[rɪˋkɔrd]**	**record your message** 錄下你的留言
tone (n.) 語氣 **[ton]**	**the proper tone of voice** 適當的語調

 track 082

Unit 8 通訊軟體（Line，2 人）

1. 情境對話

常見對話

A Please bring 3 chairs to the meeting room. There are more guests than I expected.

請拿 3 張椅子會議室，來的客人比我預期還多。

B Which meeting room are you now in?

你在哪一間會議室？

A Room 101. It is in the end of the corridor.

101室，就在走廊底。

B Right away.

馬上。

換句話說

A I'm in the meeting room, and I need you to bring 3 chairs here. It turns out more people arrived than I thought.

我正在會議室，需要你拿3張椅子過來，來的人比我想的還多。

B Please tell me the number of your meeting room.

請告訴我你的會議室號碼。

Ⓐ It is Room 101 in the end of the hallway.

就在走廊底的101室。

Ⓑ In a second.

馬上來。

2.新多益範例

(M-Br)

> Emily, has the boss come in yet? . I'am going to be late.

(W-Am)

> Not yet. The meeting started 12 minutes ago.

(M-Br)

> Please tell the boss I'll be late for the meeting.

(W-Am)

> When can you come in?

track 082

(M-Br)

It's hard to tell. My car broke down on the way to the office, and I'm still waiting for the car tow company to send a truck here.

(W-Am)

No problem. I'll let the boss know.

(M-Br)

Thank you. I know I can count on you.

（男－英）：愛蜜莉，老闆來了嗎？

（女－美）：還沒，會議12分鐘前開始了。

（男－英）：請告訴老闆我會遲到。

（女－美）：你何時會進來？

（男－英）：現在很難說，我的車在上班途中拋錨了，現在我還在等拖車公司的卡車來。

（女－美）：沒問題，我會讓老闆知道。

（男－英）：謝謝妳，我就知道我可以靠妳。

track 083

(1) What does the man contact the woman for?

(A) To report his work to the boss.

(B) To tell the boss he will be late.

(C) To ask for the office situation.

(D) To greet the visiting clients.

(1) 男子為何聯絡女子？

(A) 為了向老闆報告他的工作。

(B) 告訴老闆他會遲到。

(C) 詢問辦公室狀況。

(D) 為了歡迎來訪的客戶。

正確答案：B

(2) Why is the man not sure how late he will be?

(A) The man is waiting for the police.

(B) The man is waiting for the meeting to start.

(C) The man is waiting for the woman to arrive.

(D) The man is waiting for the tow truck.

(2) 為什麼男子不確定他會遲到多久？

(A) 男子在等警察。

(B) 男子在等會議開始。

(C) 男子在等女子到達。

(D) 男子在等拖車。

正確答案：D

 track 084

(3) **What does the man mean by saying he can "count on" the woman?**

(A) Take care.

(B) Specialize in.

(C) Rely on.

(D) Consider as.

(3) 男子説的 "**count on**" 是什麼意思？

(A) 保重。

(B) 專精於。

(C) 仰賴。

(D) 視作。

正確答案：C

3. 常見單字與片語

常見單字	片語
app(n.) 應用程式 **[æp]**	**software application** 軟體應用程式
communication (n.) 溝通；通訊 **[kə' mjunə`keʃən]**	**means of communication** 通訊工具
digital(adj.) 數位的；數字的 **[`dɪdʒɪt!]**	**a digital watch** 數字式手表
distance(n.) 距離 **[`dɪstəns]**	**distance learning** 遠距學習
instant(adj.) 立即的 **[`ɪnstənt]**	**an instant reply** 立即回覆
reply (n.) (v.) 回覆 **[rɪ`plaɪ]**	**reply to this question** 回覆這個問題
respond(v.) 作答，回答 **[rɪ`spɑnd]**	**respond to the letter** 回信
sense(v.) 感覺到，（機器）測出 **[sɛns]**	**remote sensing** 遠距感應
teleconference(n.) （透過電視電話的）電信會議 **[`tɛlɪ' kɑnfərənsɪŋ]**	**conduct the meeting by teleconference** 藉著電信會議來開會
work from home (WFH) (phr.)	**work from home during the pandemic** 疫情間在家工作

Unit 9 視訊會議（3人）

1. 情境對話

常見對話

A Did you hand in the yearly "Self-Evaluation"?
你的年度自我評量交了嗎？

B I did. Do you need any help with that?
我交了，你需要我幫你嗎？

C The questions are almost the same every year, and you just have to write some comments.
問題每年幾乎都一樣，你只要寫一點意見就好。

A I need some help with the evaluation of teamwork. Do you guys think I am a good team player?
團體合作評量這項需要點幫忙，你們覺得我是一個優秀團隊成員嗎？

B Certainly. Maybe you are just too humble to admit it.
當然，或許你只是因為謙虛而不承認。

C We all make a good team, and there is no doubt about it.
我們加起來是個好團隊，這是無庸置疑的。

track 085

換句話說

Ⓐ Are you done with the "Self-Evaluation" of the year?
你的年度自我評量完成了嗎？

Ⓑ I am. Is there anything you'd like to talk about?
完成了，有什麼你想要討論的嗎？

Ⓒ You just have to comment on the questions, which never change.
你只需要就固定不變的問題寫點意見。

Ⓐ I have some problems with teamwork performance. Have I contributed to the team very much?
我對於團隊表現這項有問題，我是否對團隊貢獻很多？

Ⓑ Of course. You should know it for sure.
當然，這一點你應該很確定。

Ⓒ Together we are a great team, and this is a fact.
我們一起是最佳團隊，這是事實。

2. 新多益範例

Jenny (W-Br): What do you think of the proposed budget of the coming year?

Michael (M-Am): Way too high, in my humble opinion.

Jason (M-Aus): It's based on the suggestions of our accounting company though.

Jenny (W-Br): Maybe we should wait and see what our manager has to say about the figures.

Michael (M-Am): You are right. As a salesperson, I wouldn't mind having a high budget.

Jason (M-Aus): Don't be too happy about it. The budget hasn't been approved yet.

珍妮（女－英）：你們覺得提議的明年經費怎麼樣？

麥可（男－美）：太高了，依我的拙見。

傑森（男－澳）：不過這是依據我們的會計部門的建議。

track 086

珍妮（女－英）：或許我們應該等著看我們經理對這數字的意見。

麥可（男－美）：你說的對，我身為業務不會抱怨經費高。

傑森（男－澳）：不要先高興，這個經費還沒有被批准。

(1) What is the general topic of the conversation?

(A) Sales performance.

(B) Budget of the next year.

(C) New staff.

(D) Accounting department.

(1) 這場對話的主要主題為何？

(A) 業績。

(B) 明年經費。

(C) 新員工。

(D) 會計部門。

正確答案：B

(2) What does the proposed budget base on?

(A) Financial experts' advice.

(B) Salespeople's requirements.

(C) Last year's sales performance.

(D) Accounting rules.

(2) 提議的經費依據為何**?**

(A) 財務專家的建議。

(B) 業務人員的要求。

(C) 去年的業績。

(D) 會計原則。

正確答案：A

(3) Why does the second man ask the first man not to be too happy now?

(A) The budget is abolished.

(B) The budget will not be approved.

(C) The budget is not realistic.

(D) The budget is not effective yet now.

(3) 為什麼第二個男子要求第一個男子現在不要太高興？

(A) 經費被刪除了。

(B) 經費不會被批准。

(C) 經費不切實際。

(D) 經費現在還未生效。

正確答案：D

track 087

3. 常見單字與片語

常見單字	片語
address (v.) 向……發表演說 [ə`drɛs]	**address the meeting** 向大會作演說
adjourn (v.) 使延期；休（會） [ə`dʒɝn]	**adjourn the meeting** 休會
concall (n.) (= conference call) 電話會議 [`kɑnkɔl]	**attend a conference call** 參加電話會議
continue (v.) 繼續 [kən`tɪnjʊ]	**continue talking in the meeting** 在會議中繼續發言
interrupt (v.) 中斷 [ˏɪntə`rʌpt]	**interrupt his talk** 中斷他的談話
schedule (n.) (v.) 安排，預定 [`skɛdʒʊl]	**schedule the meeting** 安排會議
unanimous(adj.) 一致同意的 [jʊ`nænəməs]	**unanimous conclusion** 一致的結論
video conferencing (VC) (phr.) 視訊會議 [`vɪdɪˏo ˈkɑnfərənsɪŋ]	**communicate by video** **conferencing** 用視訊會議溝通
roll call (phr.) 點名 [`rolkɔl]	**make a roll call** 點名
wrap up (phr.) 完成；結束 [`ræpʌp]	**wrap up the meeting** 總結會議

Unit 10 排除故障

1. 情境對話

常見對話

🅐 Can somebody help me? This fax machine seems to be broken.

有人可以幫幫忙嗎？傳真機似乎壞了。

🅑 It was working just a minute ago. Let me take a look.

一分鐘前還好好的，讓我看看。

🅐 Maybe I didn't operate it properly.

或許我操作有誤。

🅑 It is the loose plug, which fell out of the outlet. Someone must fix it.

是插頭鬆了，掉出了插座，該修理一下。

換句話說

🅐 Can you help me? I cannot get this fax machine working.

你可以幫我一下嗎？我無法使用這台傳真機。

🅑 A moment ago it was all right. Just let me see.

剛剛還好好的，讓我看一看。

track 088

Ⓐ Perhaps I press some wrong buttons.

或許我誤按了什麼按鈕。

Ⓑ Do you see the loose plug? Someone must repair it because it fell out of the outlet so often.

你看到了這個鬆掉的插頭嗎？老是掉出插座，該修理一下了。

2. 新多益範例

(M-Am): There seems to be some problems with our e-mailing system online.

(W-Br): What's wrong? Didn't our IT specialist just fix it a week ago?

(M-Am): Though I can receive e-mails, all my e-mails to be sent are returned.

(W-Br): That's quite serious. Why don't you call the IT expert to the office again?

(M-Am): I did, but they say the earliest time he can come in is the afternoon of the day after tomorrow.

（男－美）：我們的網路電子信箱似乎出了點問題。

（女－英）：什麼問題？我們的資訊技術專員一個星期前不是才修理過嗎？

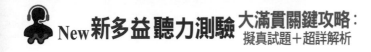 track 089

（男－美）：我雖然能夠收信，但是所有我該寄出去的電子郵件都被退回來了。

（女－英）：那很嚴重。你怎麼不叫資訊技術專員再進公司一次？

（男－美）：我有叫，但是他們說他能來的最早時間是後天下午。

(1) **What seems to cause trouble for the man?**

(A) Fax machine.

(B) E-Mail system.

(C) Telephone system.

(D) Copy machine.

(1) 男子似乎有什麼問題？

(A) 傳真機。

(B) 電子郵件系統。

(C) 電話系統。

(D) 影印機。

正確答案：B

(2) **What does the woman suggest the man to do?**

(A) To call the IT support.

(B) To contact clients by phone.

(C) To use social media.

(D) To wait and see.

track 089

(2) 女子建議男子做什麼？

(A) 叫資訊技術專員支援。

(B) 用電話聯絡客戶。

(C) 使用社群媒體。

(D) 靜觀其變。

正確答案：A

(3) Why does the man sound not so happy about the IT specialist?

(A) A client complains about not getting e-mails.

(B) The IT technician is not coming.

(C) The IT expert asks him to fix it by himself.

(D) The Tech expert will arrive but quite late.

(3) 為什麼男子聽起來對資訊技術專員不太滿意？

(A) 一位客戶抱怨沒有收到電子郵件。

(B) 資訊技術人員沒有來。

(C) 資訊技術專家要他自己修理。

(D) 技術人員很晚才會到來。

正確答案：D

 track 090

3. 常見單字與片語

常見單字	片語
budget (n.) 預算 [`bʌdʒɪt]	**be on a tight budget** 預算很緊
construction (n.) 建造 [kən`strʌkʃən]	**be under construction** 在建造中
estimate(v.) 估計；估價 [`ɛstə′ met]	**estimate the cost** 估計費用
maintenance (n.) 維修 [`mentənəns]	**road maintenance** 道路養護
order (n.) 狀況；良好的狀況 [`ɔrdɚ]	**be in good order** 狀況良好
plumber (n.) 水管工 [ˈpləmər]	**call a plumber** 叫水管工
process (n.) 過程 [`prasɛs]	**mental processes** 心理歷程
repair (v.) 修理 [rɪ`pɛr]	**repair a car** 修理一輛車
troubleshoot (v.) 檢修故障 [ˈtrʌblʃuːt]	**troubleshoot the computer** 檢修電腦
troubleshooter (n.) 檢修 [ˈtrʌblʃuːtər]	**computer troubleshooter** 電腦維修師

Unit 11 臨時派遣工

1. 情境對話

常見對話

🅐 I don't like being a temp because I don't know if I can still have the job next half of the year.

我不喜歡當臨時派遣工，因為不知道下半年是否仍然有這份工作。

🅑 You have worked as a temp for almost 5 years. I see no reason you would get fired.

你已經當派遣工幾乎有5年了，我看你不會被解職。

🅐 That's the point. They told us in the beginning there would be a chance of changing from a temp to a full-time worker.

那就是重點，開始時他們告訴我們，會有從派遣工改為全職的機會。

🅑 I wish you good luck!

我祝你好運。

 track 091

換句話說

A Being a temp worries me as I don't know what the future holds.

當臨時派遣工很令我擔心，因為我不知道未來在哪裡。

B It has been the 5th year you've worked as a temp. They would not fire you for no reason.

你當派遣工已經是第 5 年，他們不會無故將你解職的。

A You hit the sore spot. We were informed of the possibility of turning from temp into a regular worker.

你說到我的痛點了，有人告訴我們說，會有從派遣工轉為正職的機會。

B I'll keep my fingers crossed for you.

我會為你祈禱。

2. 新多益範例

(W-Am): Bryan, this afternoon six temps from the UK will come to the office. I want you to be in charge of giving them an orientation session.

track 091

(M-Br): No problem. Their main duty is to do the data entry work, and it wouldn't require much training.

(W-Am): Even though it sounds easy, it's important to let them know the company rules. May I remind you: Most of them haven't worked in a cubical in their entire lives.

(M-Br): Last year I had three young guys on their working holiday visa, and they turned out to be great assets to the company. This time I can surely take care of the British temps, too.

（女－美）：布萊恩，今天下午有 6 個從英國來的臨時派遣工會進辦公室，我希望你負責他們的職前訓練。

（男－英）：沒問題，他們的主要工作是資料輸入，不會需要太多的訓練。

（女－美）：雖然聽起來很簡單，但是讓他們明白公司規定還是很重要的，讓我提醒你：他們大部分的人一輩子不曾在辦公室隔間工作過。

（男－英）：去年我帶過工作簽證的 3 個年輕人，結果他們成為公司的優良資產，這次我一定可以帶好英國來的臨時派遣工。

 track 092

(1) What does the woman ask the man to do this afternoon?

(A) To show people around in the city.

(B) To arrange all documents.

(C) To train temporary workers from the UK.

(D) To teach young people British culture.

(1) 女子要求男子這個下午做什麼？

(A) 帶人參觀此城市。

(B) 整理所有文件。

(C) 訓練英國來的臨時派遣工。

(D) 教年輕人英國文化。

正確答案：C

(2) Why does the man think it is an easy task for the young British workers?

(A) He thinks keying in data is not hard.

(B) Their native language is English.

(C) They have worked in an office before.

(D) They are good at computer software application.

track 092

(2) 為什麼男子認為對英國來的臨時派遣工來説是件容易差事？

(A) 他認為資料輸入不難。

(B) 他們的母語是英文。

(C) 他們曾經在辦公室工作過。

(D) 他們的電腦軟體應用程式很強。

正確答案：A

(3) **What does the word "cubical" might likely mean here?**

(A) Conference room.

(B) Office space.

(C) Meeting room.

(D) Company.

(3) 這裡的 **"cubical"** 可能的意思為何？

(A) 會議室。

(B) 辦公室空間。

(C) 會議間。

(D) 公司。

正確答案：B

 track 093

3. 常見單字與片語

常見單字	片語
contract (v.) 訂約；承包 [kən`trækt]	**contract a merger** 簽約合併
cover (v.) 代替 [`kʌvɚ]	**cover for him** 替他代班
globalism (n.) 全球化 [`globəlɪzəm]	**the start of globalism** 全球化開端
outsource (v.) 將…外包 ['aʊtsɔːs]	**outsource the computing work** 外包電腦工作
remote (adj.) 遙遠的 [rɪ`mot]	**remote working** 遠距工作
shift (n.) 輪班 [ʃɪft]	**The night shift** 夜班
teamwork (n.) 團隊合作 [`tim`wɝk]	**teamwork spirit** 團隊合作精神
temp (n.) 臨時派遣工 [temp]	**a temp for the summer** 夏天的臨時工人
temping (n.) 臨時工作 ['tempɪŋ]	**a temping agency** 臨時工作仲介中心
temporary (adj.) 臨時的 [`tɛmpə′rɛrɪ]	**a temporary job** 一份臨時工作

track 093

U n i t

12 升遷

1. 情境對話

常見對話

Ⓐ I heard you are going to be promoted from the manager's secretary to office manager.
我聽說妳從總經理秘書升為辦公室經理。

Ⓑ It is just a nice position title.
那只是個好聽的職稱。

Ⓐ The promotion must come with a raise in salary, right?
這升遷一定也帶來加薪吧？

Ⓑ Really not much. Just a couple of thousand NTD.
真的不多，只有兩三千台幣。

換句話說

Ⓐ They say you become the office manager, no more being just the manager's secretary.
聽說妳成為辦公室經理了，不再只是總經理秘書。

Ⓑ It is only a change of office titles.
只是辦公室頭銜的改變。

track 093

Ⓐ Surely there is an increase in your monthly pay.

月薪一定會有增加吧？

Ⓑ To be honest, nothing worth talking about. No morethan a couple of thousand NTD.

老實說，實在不值得一提，不過只有兩三千台幣。

track 094

2. 新多益範例

(W-Am): Our manager just had a talk with me in the office.

(M-Br): Is there any good news?

(W-Am): I'll be promoted to be a sales manager and be relocated in Shanghai, and I'll have to attend a 3-month intensive training of Mandarin before going.

(M-Br): Congratulations!

(W-Am): Thank you. They say English is widely spoken there, so I wouldn't worry too much.

(M-Br): I'm sure you can make good use of what you learn in the Mandarin course. Besides, with your language talent, you will pick up the language over there very fast.

track 094

（女－美）：我們經理剛才在辦公室跟我談了一下。

（男－英）：有好消息嗎？

（女－美）：我將會被升為業務經理，要搬到上海，出發前我要上 3 個月密集普通話訓練課。

（男－英）：恭喜！

（女－美）：謝謝。聽說那兒很多人說英語，所以我不用太擔心。

（男－英）：我想你一定可以善用普通話課程所學到的知識，除此之外，你有語言天分，一定會在當地馬上學會普通話的。

(1) What is required of the woman if she wants to be promoted?

(A) To take Mandarin intensive course.

(B) To have related work experiences.

(C) To attend workshops of management.

(D) To pass the certificate exams.

(1) 女子必須要做什麼，才能夠升遷？

(A) 普通話密集課程。

(B) 具備相關工作經驗。

(C) 參加管理工作坊。

(D) 通過證照檢定考。

正確答案：A

 track 095

(2) Why does the man congratulate the woman upon?

(A) Language talent.

(B) Free flights.

(C) Mandarin improvement.

(D) Promotion.

(2) 為什麼男子恭喜女子？

(A) 語言天分。

(B) 免費機票。

(C) 普通話的進步。

(D) 升遷。

正確答案：D

(3) Why does the woman say she is not worried about the language problem?

(A) Mandarin is easy to learn.

(B) English is frequently used there.

(C) She has free Mandarin course.

(D) She has online English coaching.

(3) 為什麼女子說她不會煩惱語言問題？

(A) 普通話很容易學。

(B) 英語在那兒使用普遍。

(C) 她有免費普通話課程。

(D) 她有線上英文家教。

正確答案：B

3. 常見單字與片語

常見單字	片語
advance (v.) 發展；擢升 [əd`væns]	**her rapid advance** 她的飛速升遷
award (v.) 獎，獎品 [ə`wɔrd]	**a literary award** 文學獎
career (n.) 職業；經歷 [kə`rɪr]	**her stage career** 她的演藝職業
evaluation (n.) 評估；評價 [ɪˋvæljʊˋeʃən]	**evaluation of the project** 這個專案的評價
leadership (n.) 領導；領導才能 [`lidɚʃɪp]	**leadership of the party** 政黨領導
management (n.) 管理；經營 [`mænɪdʒmənt]	**management in this company** 這公司的管理
performance (n.) 表演；成果 [pɚˋfɔrməns]	**performance of teamwork** 團隊合作的成果
position (n.) 位置；職位 [pəˋzɪʃən]	**a managerial position** 一個管理的職位
promotion (n.) 提拔；晉升 [ˈtɛmpɪŋ]	**get a promotion** 獲得晉升
reward (v.) 酬謝；獎勵 [rɪˋwɔrd]	**reward her for her improvement** 獎勵她的進步

 track 096

Unit 13 茶水間閒聊

1. 情境對話

常見對話

A Are you heating up the frozen food in the microwave oven again?

你又在微波爐加熱冷凍食品嗎？

B It's fast and easy. I don't really have the time and money to have other food.

微波爐食品既快又方便，我實在沒有時間與金錢吃其它食品。

A Next time I can show you many options near our company, such as take-away vegetarian lunch boxes.

下次我可以帶你去看我們公司附近許多選項，像是外帶素食便當。

B Sounds just like what I need.

聽來正是我需要的。

換句話說

A I can't believe you are microwaving the frozen food once again.

真不敢相信你又在微波爐加熱冷凍食品。

track 096

B To save time and hassle. There aren't many other choices I can have around this area.

為了節省時間和麻煩。在這附近我沒什麼可以選擇的。

A Come with me tomorrow because I know where to find good lunch, such as vegetarian take-away bistro.

明天跟我一起走，因為我知道哪裡可以找到好吃午餐，例如素食外帶餐館。

B That's a great idea.

這個主意真好。

2. 新多益範例

(W-Cn): Let me show you the picture of my 3-year-old son.

(M-Br): So adorable. Do you have a nanny looking after him while you are working here?

(W-Cn): My mother looks after him. It costs too much for me to hire a professional nanny.

(M-Br): The other day I heard our boss talking about setting up a playground for the children of the employees. Hope it could soon be finished so that your son can use it.

（女－加）：看看我 3 歲兒子的照片。

（男－英）：真可愛。你在工作時間是否請了褓姆
照顧他？

（女－加）：我母親照顧他，雇用一個專業褓姆費
用太高。

（男－英）：前幾天我聽到我們老闆在談關於為員
工設立兒童遊戲場的事，希望能夠很快完工，好讓你的
兒子使用到。

(1) What are the two speakers talking about?

(A) Looking after small children.

(B) Sending kids to kindergartens.

(C) Preschool kids' developments.

(D) Joint home schooling.

(1) 他們倆在談些什麼？

(A) 照顧小小孩。

(B) 將小孩送到幼兒園。

(C) 小孩的學齡前發展。

(D) 參加家庭學校。

正確答案：A

track 097

(2) **Why is the woman's mother looking after her son?**

(A) She wants her son to stay at home.

(B) She prefers her own family members to do it.

(C) She cannot find any good nursery school.

(D) She cannot afford to hire a nanny.

(2) 為什麼女子的母親照顧她的兒子？

(A) 她想要她的兒子待在家。

(B) 她想要自己家人照顧他。

(C) 她不能找到任何好的托兒所。

(D) 她無法負擔請褓姆。

正確答案：D

(3) **What does the man tell the woman about the new project about the employees' children?**

(A) A professional babysitter will stand by.

(B) A child psychologist will be hired.

(C) A children's playground is being planned.

(D) An after-school teacher is coming here.

(3) 男子告訴女子什麼關於員工小孩的新專案？

(A) 一位專業褓姆會準備待命。

(B) 會僱用一位兒童心理學家。

(C) 正在建兒童遊戲區。

(D) 一位課後老師會過來。

正確答案：C

 track 098

3. 常見單字與片語

常見單字	片語
advice (n.) 勸告，忠告 [əd`vaɪs]	**a piece of advice** 一個忠告
advise (v.) 勸告 [əd`vaɪz]	**advise her to wait** 勸她等待
chat (n.) 職業；經歷 [tʃæt]	**have a friendly chat** 友善聊天
consult(v.) 諮詢 [kən`sʌlt]	**consult him about the application** 向他諮詢申請之事
gossip (n.) 流言蜚語 [`gɑsəp]	**have a gossip with the neighbors** 跟鄰居聊八卦
remind (v.) 提醒 [rɪ`maɪnd]	**remind him of his promise** 提醒他曾許下的諾言
reveal(v.) 透露 [rɪ`vil]	**reveal the secret** 透露秘密
rumor(n.) 謠言 [`rumɚ]	**a rumor about a managerial position** 一個關於管理職位的謠言
socialize(v.) 社交；交際 [`soʃəˈlaɪz]	**socialize with salespeople** 跟業務社交
support(v.) 支持 [sə`port]	**support each other** 彼此支持

track 099

4 簡短獨白

Directions: You will hear some talks given by a single speaker. You will be asked to answer three questions about what the speaker says in each talk. Select the best response to each question and mark the letter (A), (B), (C), or (D) on your answer sheet. The talks will not be printed in your test book and will be spoken only one time.

解說：你會聽到幾段一個人的獨白，你必須要回答關於每段獨白的三個問題，請選出每個問題的最佳答案，然後在答案紙上劃記(A)或 (B) 或(C)或 (D)，這些獨白不會在測驗本上印出來，而且只會播放一次。

範例

71. What does the speaker say about the repair?

(A) It is not required.

(B) It has been finished early.

(C) It will be inexpensive.

(D) It is covered by a warranty.

71. 說話者說了些什麼關於修理的事？

(A) 沒有這個需要。

(B) 提前完成了。

track 099

(C) 不會太貴。

(D) 保固維修。

72. When can the listener pick up his car?

(A) Today.

(B) Tomorrow.

(C) Next week.

(D) In two weeks.

72. 聽者什麼時候可以來取車？

(A) 今天。

(B) 明天。

(C) 下星期。

(D) 兩星期後。

73. What does the speaker offer to do?

(A) Look for a used part.

(B) Refund the cost of a charge.

(C) Send an invoice.

(D) Arrange a ride.

73. 說話者提供了什麼服務？

(A) 尋找一個用過的零件。

(B) 退還一筆費用。

(C) 送貨品明細表。

(D) 安排接送。

正確選項：71. (B)；72. (B)；73. (D)

track 100

獨白中譯

Hello, Mr. Lee, this is Thomas from BKS Auto Shop calling with some information about your car repair. I know we told you that it would take until next week to get the part we ordered, but we got the part early, and I was able to finish the repair. We are going to be closing for the day in a few minutes, but you are welcome to come get your car anytime tomorrow. If you need a ride tomorrow to our shop tomorrow, let me know, and I can arrange one for you.

李先生您好，我是BKS 汽車修理廠的湯瑪斯，想要告訴您關於您車子修理的事項，我知道曾經告訴您說，要到下星期才能得到我們訂的零件，但是我們提前得到了，所以車子提前修理完畢，我們今天再過幾分鐘就要打烊了，不過歡迎您明天任何時候來取車，如果您需要我們安排明天來這裡的接送，請告訴我，我好幫您安排。

1. 注意重點

作答要訣在於，在獨白播放前要先瀏覽 3 個問題與選項，如果沒有時間略讀完 4 個選項，也要掃讀關鍵字，如此才能於聆聽播音前心理先做預先準備，答題時才能增加答對的機率，並且大幅節省答題時間；結束了

一段獨白與 3 個問題後，於下一段獨白開始前，一定要預先瀏覽其下 3 個問題與選項，以此順序與節奏作答下去。

　　這個英語獨白部分經常出現於工商企業，程度並不會太難，只是對於不常做聽力練習的人來說，可能因為速度和專注力的緣故，變成了一大挑戰，建議平時就不妨將多益聽力錄音反覆練習聽，甚至跟讀，做聽寫，等累積了一定程度後，就能夠跟上CNN和BBC新聞，一邊增進英語能力，一邊了解世界大事。

2. 出題類型

問內容概要：主題＆大意	**What…about?**
問內容概要：說話者與聽者	**Who…?**
問內容概要：場所	**Where…?**

問內容事物細節	**What…?**
問內容人物細節	**Who…?**
問內容地點細節	**Where…?**
問內容時間細節	**When…?**
問內容原因細節	**Why…?**
問內容方式細節	**How…?**

track 101

1.第一型題目　問內容概要：

(1) 問主題與目的

　　通常獨白內容前後順序的發展是固定的，一開始就會將主題或目的簡要提出，然後才會帶出細節，所以要注意聆聽開頭的部分，以掌握內容主要大意。

例句

例 What is the main topic of the talk?
這段話的主題是什麼？

例 What is the short talk mainly about?
這段簡短談話主要是關於什麼？

例 What is the announcement about?
這段廣播是關於什麼？

(2) 問內容概要：說話者與聽者

　　說話者的身分職位與主題非常有關，通常可以於獨白一開始的地方找到答案線索。

　　要得知聽者身分，因為聽眾不會於獨白中出現，則需要綜合說話者身分職位與獨白內容，才能確定正在聽這段獨白者可能為何人。

例句

例 Who is most likely the speaker?
誰最有可能是說話者？

track 101

例 Who is probably the speaker of the announcement?
這段廣播可能是誰說的？

例 Who probably leaves the message?
誰可能是留話的人？

例 Who is most likely the audience?
誰最可能是聽眾？

例 Who are probably the listeners of this short talk?
這段簡短談話的聽者可能是誰？

(3) 問內容概要：場所

這種題型主要是要問該演講或可能於哪裡舉行，獨白也可能是廣播的播音或電話答錄機的錄音，通常這類的答案不會於獨白的內容中出現，與聽者身分題目一樣，必須綜合所有的線索來推論出可能的正確答案。

例句

例 Where does the speech most likely take place?
這場演講最可能在哪裡舉行？

例 Where is the announcement probably being made?
這段廣播可能在哪裡播放？

例 Where is possibly the short talk taking place?
這段簡短談話可能在哪裡發生？

track 102

第二型題目　問內容細節：5 W 1 H

---

(1) 內容事物細節

What…?

例句

例 What is the topic of the meeting?
會議的主題是什麼？

(2) 內容人物細節

Who…?

例句

例 Who will probably host the meeting?
誰可能會主持會議？

(3) 內容地點細節

Where…?

例句

例 Where will the meeting probably take place?
會議可能會在什麼地方舉行？

(4) 內容時間細節

When…?

例句

例 When will the meeting start?
會議什麼時候會開始？

(5) 內容原因細節

Why…?

例句

例 Why will they have a meeting?
他們為什麼要舉行會議？

(6) 內容方式細節

How…?

例句

例 How will they hold the meeting?
他們要如何舉行會議？

新制新多益增加圖表：價目表，火車時刻表，辦公室安排配置等等，有時要簡單算數與推理。

3. 常見場景

Unit 1 電話留言
Unit 2 電台廣播
Unit 3 廣告宣傳
Unit 4 公司內部公告
Unit 5 機場和飛機內的廣播
Unit 6 會議發言
Unit 7 活動解說
Unit 8 人物介紹
Unit 9 觀光導覽
Unit 10 講解流程

各項常見場景之下先舉獨白範例，然後就常見題目，聽寫＆跟讀，常見片語與句型來一一探討：

符號註解：

Am＝美國

Cn＝加拿大

Br＝英國

Aus＝澳洲

 track 103

Unit 1 電話留言

　　電話留常見於公司語音服務，其中以服務業者的自動留言系統最為常見，包含預約、取消預約、變更預約等等，除此之外，留言給不在位子上的員工也很常見，可能是公司給個人，或是客戶給個人，內容多與公司內部管理或個人負責業務相關。

電話留言例題

先解題

1. Why is the speaker calling?

(A) For informing the other of an application procedure.

(B) For applying for a reimbursement.

(C) For applying to travel to Tokyo.

(D) For reporting a business trip overseas.

1. 說話者為什麼打電話來？

(A) 為了告知對方申請程序。

(B) 為了申請款項。

(C) 為了申請去東京旅遊。

(D) 為了報導海外出差。

正確答案：A

2. What does the speaker want to remind the other?

   (A) There will be a meeting to discuss it.

   (B) A schedule of the business trip is needed.

   (C) Entertaining clients should not be included.

   (D) All receipts are required for the application for reimbursement.

2. 說話者想要提醒對方什麼？

   (A) 會有一個討論這個的會議。

   (B) 需要一個商務之旅的行程表。

   (C) 不應該包含與客戶的交際費。

   (D) 申報費用需要所有的收據。

正確答案：D

3. What kind of receipts does the speaker especially emphasize?

   (A) Business.

   (B) Entertainment.

   (C) Transportation.

   (D) Accommodation.

3. 說話者特別強調什麼樣的收據？

   (A) 商務。

   (B) 交際。

   (C) 交通。

   (D) 住宿。

正確答案：B

● 獨白內文請見(4)跟讀

(1) 解析常見題目

大意

What is the main subject of the message?
這段留言內容的主題為何？

Why is the person calling?
這個人打電話的目的為何？

What does the person leave a message for?
這個人為何留言？

內容細節

Why does the man want to change the appointment?
為什麼這男士想要改變約定時間？

What does the man want the woman do immediately?
這男士想要女士立刻做什麼？

What is probably the woman's position in the company?
這女士在公司裡的指稱可能為何？

When will the man call again?
男士何時會再來電？

track 105

(2) 常見句子

Hi, this is the Whole Food Supermarket leaving a message for Mr. Jason Liu.
嗨，這裡是全食物超市，想要留話給劉傑森。

The microwave oven he ordered the day before yesterday just arrived.
前天訂的微波爐剛送到。

We will keep the microwave oven for him for 7 days for him at the service counter.
我們會為他將微波爐在服務台保留7天。

If there is any questions, please call us at (02) 2971 2541. Thank you for shopping here.
如果有任何問題，請來電(02) 2971 2541，謝謝光臨。

(3) 聽寫（英國口音）

1. Hello, this is Jenny from the _____ Department.
   您好，這裡是財務部門的珍妮。

2. I am calling to let you know I've received the _____ of the reimbursement of your business trip to Tokyo in July.
   我打電話來是要告訴您我已經收到了您七月到東京出差的請款申請。

track 105

3. May I remind you that it is our company policy that all valid _____ are required for the application.

   容我提醒您，公司規定要請款時必須附上所有合法收據。

4. You've not _____ all the valid receipts, especially those of entertainment.

   您還有些收據還沒交上，特別是交際費。

5. Please _____ the copies of the receipts to me by this Friday.

   請在這星期五前將所有收據影本交上。

6. Thank you very much.

   非常謝謝您。

答案：

1. Finance
2. application
3. receipts
4. submitted
5. hand in

track 106

(4) 跟讀（英國口音）

Hello, this is Jenny from the Finance Department. I am calling to let you know I've received the application of the reimbursement of your business trip to Tokyo in July. May I remind you that it is our company policy that all valid receipts are required for the application. You've not submitted all the valid receipts, especially those of entertainment. Please hand in the copies of the receipts to me by this Friday. Thank you very much.

您好，這裡是財務部門的珍妮。我打電話來是要告訴您我已經收到了您七月到東京出差的請款申請。容我提醒您，公司規定要請款時必須附上所有合法收據。您還有些收據還沒交上，特別是交際費。請在這星期五前將所有收據影本交上。非常感謝您。

(5) 常見片語與句型

常見片語	常見句型
after the beep 嗶聲後	**Please leave a message after the beep.** 請於嗶聲後留言。
at the moment 現在	**He is not in at the moment.** 他現在不在這裡。
be (not) available 有空／沒空	**He is not available right now.** 他現在沒空。
go back to 回覆	**I'll get back to you as soon as possible.** 我會儘快回覆您。
leave a good impression on 留下良好印象	**Your message left a good impression on the interviewer.** 你的留言給面試官留下了良好印象。
leave a message 留話，留下訊息	**Would you like to leave a message for him?** 您想要留話給他嗎？
make sure 確認	**Make sure you leave your name and phone number in your message.** 確定你留下了你的名字與電話號碼。
talk to you later 晚點再跟你說	**I'll talk to you later.** 我晚點再跟你說。
Thank you for… 謝謝您……	**Thank you for calling us to let us know.** 謝謝您打電話來讓我們知道。
Would you mind…? 您是否介意……？	**Would you mind calling me back?** 您是否介意回電話給我？

track 107

Unit 2 電台廣播

　　電台廣播內容可能是關於交通事故、地震、火災等突發狀況，也可能是氣象預報、廣告工商時間等等，重點在於專注聽報導內容關鍵字，還有日期、時間或價格的數字。

電台廣播例題

先解題

1. What is this announcement mainly about?

(A) Radio talk show.

(B) Weather prediction.

(C) Traffic report.

(D) First aid.

1. 這段廣播主題為何？

(A) 電台脫口秀。

(B) 天氣預報。

(C) 交通路況報導。

(D) 急救措施。

正確答案：C

2. **What is NOT one of the main causes of the traffic jam?**

(A) The traffic accident with a truck and a car.

(B) People are waiting for the police and first aid people.

(C) Bad weather with a thunderstorm.

(D) The Airport MRT route.

2. 下列何者不是造成此交通阻塞的原因？

(A) 貨車與小客車的交通事故。

(B) 人們在等警方和急救人員到場。

(C) 雷震雨壞天氣。

(D) 機捷路線。

正確答案：D

3. **What' the advice here for the drivers who haven't departed?**

(A) Taking public transportation system.

(B) Waiting for the weather to get better.

(C) Avoiding going to Taipei.

(D) Contacting the police first.

3. 這裡給還未上路的駕駛的建議為何？

(A) 使用大眾運輸系統。

(B) 等待天氣好轉。

(C) 避免去台北。

(D) 先聯絡警方。

正確答案：A

track 108

●獨白內文請見(4)跟讀

(1) 解析常見題目

大意

What is the main topic of the news report?
這新聞報導的主題為何？

What is the radio host mainly talking about?
廣播電台主播主要在談什麼？

What is the radio host's general tone?
這個主播的大致語氣為何？

內容細節

When will the traffic probably be back to normal?
交通何時會轉為正常？

What are on sale during the Africa Festival?
什麼物品在非洲節慶特賣？

What does the host advise the listeners to do?
主播建議聽眾做什麼？

What is going to come after this news report?
新聞報導之後會有什麼活動？

track 108

(2) 常見句子

Hello, this is Susan from FM 95, and I'll be with you for the following 1.5 hours.

哈囉，這裡是FM 95 的蘇珊，接下來的一小時半我會與您共度。

Today is the extra working day on Saturday for the long weekend next week, so let's start with some refreshing music.

今天是星期六補班日，為了下周末的連假，讓我們用振奮的音樂來作開始。

You are welcome to call in and tell me what songs you'd like to listen to.

歡迎打電話進來點想聽的歌。

As long as I can find it, I will play your music to accompany you working this afternoon.

只要我找得到，就會播給您聽，陪伴您度過這個下午。

(3) 聽寫（美國口音）

1. This is Richard from News 2.0, and I'd like to _____ you traffic from Linkou to Taipei is right now bumper to bumper.

這是News 2.0 電台的李察，想要提醒您從林口到台北市的交通非常擁擠。

track 109

2. A huge thunderstorm started half an hour ago and has caused poor _____ .

半小時前開始下大雷雨，導致能見度相當差。

3. A serious traffic accident _____ a car and a truck happened about 10 minutes ago.

十分鐘前發生了一場轎車與卡車的嚴重車禍。

4. The police and the _____ haven't arrived yet at the scene, and that causes a delay in rescuing the wounded.

到現在警察與消防車隊還沒有到達現場，造成了延誤傷者就醫。

5. Those who haven't gone on the highway and wish to arrive Taipei without delay had better _____ taking the Taoyuan Airport MRT.

還未上高速公路，想要準時到達台北市的人，最好考慮搭乘桃園機場捷運。

答案：

1. remind
2. visibility
3. involving
4. ambulance
5. consider

track 109

(4) 跟讀（美國口音）

This is Richard from News 2.0, and I'd like to remind you traffic from Linkou to Taipei is right now bumper to bumper. A huge thunderstorm started half an hour ago and has caused poor visibility. A serious traffic accident involving a car and a truck happened about 10 minutes ago. The police and the ambulance haven't arrived yet at the scene, and that causes a delay in rescuing the wounded. Those who haven't gone on the highway and wish to arrive Taipei without delay had better consider taking the Taoyuan Airport MRT.

這是News 2.0 電台的李察，想要提醒您從林口到台北市的交通非常擁擠。半小時前開始下大雷雨，導致能見度相當差。十分鐘前發生了一場轎車與卡車的嚴重車禍。到現在警察與消防車隊還沒有到達現場，造成了延誤傷者就醫。還未上高速公路，想要準時到達台北市的人，最好考慮搭乘桃園機場捷運。

track 110

(5) 常見片語與句型

常見片語	常見句型
call in 現場直播，並開放讓觀眾打電話進來	**Welcome to call in during the next 15 minutes.** 接下來的 **15** 分鐘歡迎觀眾打電話進來。
live stream 直播	**She is the streamer in the live stream.** 她是這個直播節目的直播主。
placement marketing 置入性行銷	**This song seems to contain placement marketing of a famous brand.** 這首歌似乎含有名牌的置入性行銷。
play a gig （尤指演奏現代或流行樂的）表演	**Many young singers play the first gig on YouTube.** 很多年輕歌手的第一次表演是在 **YouTube**。
radio host 廣播主持人	**Many radio hosts speak fluent English.** 很多廣播主持人會說流利英語。
special offer 特價	**We'll have all sorts of items on special offer for the Lunar New Year.** 我們會有各種因應農曆年節的特價品。
special request 特別要求	**Please let us know your special request for the special one.** 請讓我們知道你為你特別的人的特別要求。
tune in 收聽	**Tune in tomorrow at the same time!** 請在明天同一時間繼續收聽！
weather forecast 氣象預報	**The weather forecast said that it would snow in Taiwan tomorrow.** 氣象預報說台灣明天會下雪。

track 110

Unit 3 廣告宣傳

　　廣告宣傳經常出現於超市、大賣場、園遊會等等場所，除了對於特賣時間、地點訊息的關鍵字要特別注意外，關於折扣等價格問題更是重點。

廣告宣傳例題

先解題

1. Who is the announcement for?

　(A) Chefs.

　(B) Farmers.

　(C) Shoppers.

　(D) Employees.

1. 這段廣播是要播給誰聽的？

　(A) 主廚。

　(B) 農友。

　(C) 購物者。

　(D) 員工。

正確答案：C

track 111

2. What should the customers do in order to win a return ticket to New Zealand?

　(A) Leave name and telephone numbers.

track 111

(B) Buy an item and then draw lots.

(C) Become a member of the promotion.

(D) Have a conversation with the chef.

2. 消費者需要做什麼才能贏得到紐西蘭的來回機票？

(A) 留下名字和電話號碼。

(B) 購買一樣商品，然後抽獎。

(C) 成為促銷的一員。

(D) 與主廚對話。

正確答案：B

3. What is the special guest especially knowledgeable about?

(A) Fresh mixed fruit juice.

(B) Promotion activity.

(C) Cooking without meat.

(D) Information of food ingredients.

3. 這位特別來賓對於哪方面特別專長？

(A) 鮮榨果汁。

(B) 促銷活動。

(C) 無肉料理。

(D) 食材資訊。

正確答案：D

獨白內文請見(4)跟讀

(1) 解析常見題目

大意

What is the main subject of the announcement?
這段廣播的主題是什麼？

What is the woman mainly talking about?
這女子主要在談什麼？

What is going to happen in 20 minutes?
接下來的20分鐘會發生什麼事？

內容細節

What are going to be on sale in 20 minutes?
接下來的20分鐘有什麼特賣？

Who are able to get 50% off?
什麼人可以得到半價優惠？

How can customers get coupons?
顧客要怎麼樣才能得到折價券？

Where is the special show of kitchenware going to take place?
廚具特展將會在哪裡舉行？

track 112

(2) 常見句子

Hi, today is the opening day of Billy's Bakery and we offer one free cupcake for the customers the whole day.

嗨，今天是比利烘焙坊的開幕日，我們一整天提供顧客免費杯子蛋糕。

Our choices of cupcakes will blow your mind, featuring the special mango and kiwi flavors.

我們的杯子蛋糕選項會讓您驚豔，主打特別芒果和奇異果口味。

For all other baked products, we have 30% for all bread products and 20% for all cakes.

至於其它的烘焙產品，麵包都打七折，蛋糕都打八折。

You wouldn't want to miss this opportunity, so come and check it out!

千萬不要錯過這個機會，快來看一看！

(3) 聽寫（澳洲口音）

1. Good afternoon, everyone, we are now having a special _____ of a series of agricultural produce from New Zealand.

大家午安，我們現在要進行一系列紐西蘭產品的特促銷。

track 112

2. Anyone who _____ an item in this special section can take part in the lucky draw to win a return ticket to Auckland.

只要來這個特別專櫃消費的人都可以參加奧克蘭機票抽獎。

3. Please do come by and taste our mixed juice of _____ fruits from New Zealand, including kiwis, of course.

請一定要來這兒嚐嚐紐西蘭綜合水果汁，當然包含奇異果在內。

4. You can have a friendly chat with our special guest from Wellington, who is a professional chef, and ask him about all the questions about food _____.

您可以與我們來自威靈頓的特別來賓隨意聊聊，他是一位專業廚師，可以向他請教各種關於食材的問題。

5. This promotion activity only _____ until this Sunday, which means only 3 days to go, including today.

這個促銷活動只到星期日為止，包括今天只剩 3 天。

答案：

1. promotion
2. purchases
3. various
4. ingredients
5. lasts

track 113

(4) 跟讀（澳洲口音）

Good afternoon, everyone, we are now having a special promotion of a series of agricultural produce from New Zealand. Anyone who purchases an item in this special section can take part in the lucky draw to win a return ticket to Auckland.

Please do come by and taste our mixed juice of various fruits from New Zealand, including kiwis, of course. You can have a friendly chat with our special guest from Wellington, who is a professional chef, and ask him about all the questions about food ingredients. This promotion activity only lasts until this Sunday, which means only 3 days to go, including today.

大家午安，我們現在要進行一系列紐西蘭產品的特促銷，只要來這個特別專櫃消費的人都可以參加奧克蘭機票抽獎，請一定要來這兒嚐嚐紐西蘭綜合水果汁，當然包含奇異果在內。您可以與我們來自威靈頓的特別來賓隨意聊聊，他是一位專業廚師，可以向他請教各種關於食材的問題。這個促銷活動只到星期日為止，包括今天只剩 3 天。

(5) 常見片語與句型

常見片語	常見句型
catchy slogan 好記的廣告台詞	**A catchy slogan catches the attention of people and is easy to remember.** 一個好聽易記的廣告台詞吸引人注意，而且留在人們腦海裡。
discounted price 折扣價	**Many customers are attracted to the discounted prices in the store.** 很多消費者被店裡的折扣價所吸引。
food sampling 試吃	**Our food sampling of tofu products is now on.** 我們正在進行豆腐試吃活動。
line up 排隊	**At least 20 customers lined up in front of the new cafeteria for the special offer.** 至少有 20 位顧客在新開的餐館前排隊買特價餐點。
new arrival 新到商品	**Please take a look at the new arrival of the spring items.** 請看看新到的春季商品。
sales strategy 銷售策略	**Many business owners try to come up with effective sales strategies.** 很多生意人努力發想有效的銷售策略。

track 114

Unit 4 公司內部公告

公司內部公告通常是用播音方式，可能是公司提醒員工要例行開會或臨時有訪客等事項，通常都是關於公司或辦公室等用語。

公司內部公告例題

先解題

1. **What is the topic of the announcement?**

    (A) Computer maintenance.

    (B) An IT training session.

    (C) A typing test.

    (D) Data protection.

1. 這段廣播的主題為何？

    (A) 電腦維修。

    (B) 資訊科技訓練課程。

    (C) 打字測驗。

    (D) 數據保護。

正確答案：B

2. **What does the speaker want the listeners to prepare a set of username and password for?**

    (A) To set up a bank account.

    (B) To log on a website.

(C) To give feedback.

(D) To access a database.

2. 為何說話者要聽者準備一組帳號和密碼？

(A) 為了設立一個銀行帳戶。

(B) 為了登入一個網頁。

(C) 為了提供回饋。

(D) 為了進入一個資料庫。

正確答案：D

3. What are the listeners expected to be able to do the next day?

(A) To attend a workshop.

(B) To key in data.

(C) To pass a test.

(D) To get certified.

3. 聽者第二天必須要會做什麼？

(A) 參加工作坊。

(B) 輸入數據。

(C) 通過測驗。

(D) 通過認證。

正確答案：C

track 115

● 獨白內文請見(4)跟讀

(1) 解析常見題目

大意

What is the announcement mainly about?
這段廣播主要內容為何？

Why is the manager making this announcement?
經理為何廣播？

What does the speaker want the listeners to do now?
說話者要聽眾做什麼？

內容細節

Where are the staff members going to meet right now?
工作人員現在集合要做什麼？

What is going to be the discussed in the meeting?
會議將要討論什麼？

What does the manager ask the staff members to gather in front of the entrance for?
經理要求員工在門口集合做什麼？

What are the listeners most likely to do next?
聽眾接下來最可能做什麼？

track 115

(2) 常見句子

Attention everyone: In 30 minutes, the Health Check-up Car will arrive in front of our gym.
大家注意：再過30分鐘，健檢車會來到我們健身中心門口。

All employees in the gym have to undertake this yearly check-up, including service clerks and coaches.
所有的健身中心員工都要做年度例行健康檢查，包含服務人員與教練。

The results of the check-up will be mailed to your contact addresses with registered mail in one week.
健康檢查的結果會在一星期內掛號郵寄到你的聯絡地址。

In case you have any questions, please direct them to the two nurses at the service desk later.
如果你有任何問題，請等一下向服務台的兩位護理師請教。

(3) 聽寫（美國口音）

 track 116

1. Attention employees: An IT specialist is coming this afternoon to hold a special training _____ at 2 pm, which all of you are required to attend.

track 116

各位員工請注意，一位資訊技術專員今天下午兩點會過來舉行一個特別訓練，你們都必須要參加。

2. This IT trainer is going to _____ how to navigate the new website of our company and, most important of all, how to access our database.

這位特別的資管講師將會展示如何瀏覽我們公司的新網站，最重要的，如何進入我們的資料庫。

3. Please prepare a set of username and password because each of you has to _____ an account.

請準備一組使用者名稱與密碼，因為你們每個人都必須申請一個帳號。

4. Please pay special attention because there will be a _____ in the end of the training.

請特別專心，因為訓練結束後會有一個測驗。

5. From tomorrow on, you are all expected to begin the work of data _____.

明天起，你們都要能夠開始做資料分析的工作。

6. Thank you for your _____.

謝謝大家。

答案：

1. session

2. demonstrate

track 116

3. register

4. quiz

5. analysis

6. attention

(4) 跟讀（美國口音）

Attention employees: An IT specialist is coming this afternoon to hold a special training session at 2 pm, which all of you are required to attend. This IT trainer is going to demonstrate how to navigate the new website of our company and, most important of all, how to access our database. Please prepare a set of username and password because each of you has to register an account. Please pay special attention because there will be a quiz in the end of the training. From tomorrow on, you are all expected to begin the work of data analysis. Thank you for your attention.

各位員工請注意，一位資訊技術專員今天下午兩點會過來舉行一個特別訓練，你們都必須要參加，這位特別的資管講師將會展示如何瀏覽我們公司的新網站，最重要的，如何進入我們的資料庫。請準備一組使用者名稱與密碼，因為你們每個人都必須申請一個帳號。請特別專心，因為訓練結束後會有一個測驗，明天起，你們都要能夠開始做資料分析的工作。謝謝大家。

track 117

(5) 常見片語與句型

常見片語	常見句型
big data 大數據	**Because of big data, business owners can analyze their customers much faster than before.** 很多老闆因為大數據而能比從前更快分析顧客群。
company policy 公司政策	**It is our company policy to require advance payment before shipment.** 我們公司規定裝貨運前要先付款。
make adjustments to 調整	**She made some adjustments to the schedule.** 她調整了時間表。
make it known that… 宣布	**We made it known that our company has nothing to do with it.** 我們公司宣布與此無關。
open house 開放參觀日	**We will host an open house to invite the public to visit our cake factory.** 我們會舉辦開放參觀日，邀請大家來參觀我們的蛋糕工廠。
pay attention to 注意	**Please pay attention to the new announcement.** 請注意新告示。

Unit 5 機場和飛機內的廣播

　　機場廣播經常出現於新多益考題，通常是班機延誤或取消等訊息，只要注意聽關鍵字，不會有太大問題；飛機內的廣播也偶爾會以機長廣播方式出現，內容相對機場廣播而言簡單許多。

機場和飛機內的廣播例題

先解題

1. Where does the announcement most likely take place?

(A) On a crew boat.

(B) On an airplane.

(C) On a helicopter.

(D) On a tourist bus.

1. 這段廣播最可能在哪裡播放的？

(A) 在船上。

(B) 在飛機上。

(C) 在直升機上。

(D) 在觀光巴士上。

正確答案：B

track 118

2. What is urgently looked for at the moment?

    (A) A stewardess.

    (B) A care-giver.

    (C) A pilot.

    (D) A doctor.

2. 現在急著尋找何種人？

    (A) 空服員。

    (B) 看護。

    (C) 機長。

    (D) 醫師。

正確答案：D

3. Why is it not easy to know the passenger's physical condition?

    (A) He has no travel companions.

    (B) He does not tell others about it.

    (C) He has not been feeling like this before.

    (D) He does not admit he is ill.

3. 為什麼要知道這位乘客的身體狀況不容易？

    (A) 他沒有旅伴。

    (B) 他沒有告訴別人這件事。

    (C) 他之前沒有這種狀況。

    (D) 他不承認他有病。

正確答案：A

●獨白內文請見(4)跟讀

(1) 解析常見題目

大意

What is the announcement mainly about?
這段廣播的內容主題為何？

Why is the airlines company making this announcement?
為何航空公司放這段廣播？

What does the speaker want the passengers to do now?
說話者想要乘客做什麼？

內容細節

When is the next flight going to take off?
下一班飛機什麼時候起飛？

Where should passengers go to change their flights?
乘客需要去哪裡改班機？

How can the passengers know if the next flight would take off on time?
乘客要怎樣知道下一班機會準時起飛？

What are the passengers most likely to do after the announcement?
乘客在聽到廣播後最有可能做什麼？

track 119

(2) 常見句子

All passengers onboard, in a few minutes we'll be landing on the Frankfurt Airport.
所有乘客請注意，再過幾分鐘我們就會抵達法蘭克福機場。

The local weather is nice and shiny, a typical summer day.
當地氣候溫暖有陽光，是夏天常見天氣。

This has been a smooth flight, and it has been my pleasure to be your captain.
整躺旅程非常平穩，我很榮幸能擔任你們的機長。

Please don't forget your personal belongings and thank you for flying with the China Airlines.
請不要忘記帶走隨身行李，感謝您搭乘華航。

(3) 聽寫（澳洲口音）

1. All _____, may I have your attention, please?
   所有乘客請注意。

2. If there is a medical doctor or nurse _____, please contact one of our flight crew members.
   如果機上有醫師或護理師，請與機組人員聯絡。

track 119

3. One passenger is feeling lightheaded and having extreme _____, and he seems to be about to vomit and faint.

有一位乘客感到頭暈，而且極度不舒服，他似乎快要嘔吐昏倒。

4. We urgently need _____ from medical specialists.

我們急需醫療專家的協助。

5. Since he is traveling alone, we don't know if he has any illnesses or _____.

因為他單獨搭乘飛機，我們無從得知他是否有任何疾病或症狀。

6. Your help would be greatly _____. Thanks very much.

我們感謝您的協助。謝謝大家。

答案：

   1. passengers

   2. onboard

   3. discomfort

   4. assistance

   5. conditions

   6. appreciated

track 120

(4) 跟讀（澳洲口音）

All passengers, may I have your attention, please? If there is a medical doctor or nurse onboard, please contact one of our flight crew members. One passenger is feeling lightheaded and having extreme discomfort, and he seems to be about to vomit and faint. We urgently need assistance from medical specialists. Since he is traveling alone, we don't know if he has any illnesses or conditions. Your help would be greatly appreciated. Thanks very much.

所有乘客請注意，如果機上有醫師或護理師，請與機組人員聯絡，有一位乘客感到頭暈，而且極度不舒服，他似乎快要嘔吐昏倒，我們急需醫療專家的協助，因為他單獨搭乘飛機，我們無從得知他是否有任何疾病或症狀。我們感謝您的協助，謝謝大家。

track 120

(5) 常見片語與句型

常見片語	常見句型
carry-on luggage 隨身行李	**What is considered carry-on luggage?** 什麼算是隨身行李？
emergency case 緊急狀況	**Citizens who face any emergency case of COVID-19 can call 1922.** 國人遇到任何關於新冠肺炎的緊急狀況可以撥打 **1922**。
fear of flying 搭飛機的恐懼	**She tries to get over fear of flying.** 她試著克服搭飛機的恐懼。
flight attendant 空服員	**Recently many flight attendants lost their jobs due to COVID-19.** 因為新冠肺炎很多飛行員失業了。
get on/get off 登機／下飛機	**This morning my boss got on the plane in the Texas to attend a meeting in Boston.** 今早我的老闆於德州搭機去波士頓開會。
land on 降落於	**We are going to land on Tokyo in a few minutes.** 再過幾分鐘我們將要降落於東京。

track 121

6 會議發言

　　會議上的長篇發言，就像是Part 3 對話一樣，只是由一人發表言論，長度較長，而且沒有對方的回應而已。

會議發言例題

先解題

1. What is the speaker's purpose of having a meeting here?

(A) Announcing new regulations.

(B) Listening to the employees' feedback.

(C) Showing new office robots.

(D) Familiarizing himself with the office.

1. 這位說話者在這裡開這個會的目的為何？

(A) 發表新規定。

(B) 聆聽員工的回饋。

(C) 展示新辦公室機器人。

(D) 熟悉辦公室。

正確答案：B

2. How long has it been since the merge?

(A) Less than 1 year.

(B) Exactly 1 year.

(C) More than 1 year.

(D) Not mentioned here.

track 121

2. 公司合併後有多久了？

(A) 少於一年。

(B) 剛好一年。

(C) 多於一年。

(D) 這裡沒有提及。

正確答案：C

3. What is the first topic they are going to discuss?

(A) Work spaces.

(B) Workloads.

(C) Work rules.

(D) Work uniforms.

3. 他們將要討論的第一個主題為何？

(A) 工作空間。

(B) 工作量。

(C) 工作規則。

(D) 工作制服。

正確答案：A

●獨白內文請見(4)跟讀

(1) 解析常見題目

大意

track 122

What is the speaker making the statement for?
發言者為什麼要發言？

What is the purpose for them to meet here?
他們在這裡會面的目的是什麼？

Who are the listeners most likely to be?
聽眾最可能是什麼人？

內容細節

What is probably the occasion for them to get together?
他們會面可能是因為什麼原因？

What contract are they going to agree on?
他們將同意要簽什麼合約？

Why is the attendance very important?
為什麼出席率很重要？

Where are they probably going to meet next time?
他們下次可能要在什麼地方會面？

(2) 常見句子

On behalf of our CEO, I'd like to announce that we will have one-week trip to Vietnam, starting on September 28.
我代表執行長宣布我們從 9 月 28 日開始為期一星期的越南之旅。

We have arranged this company tour with the King's Travel Agency.
我們是透過國王旅行社安排這趟公司員工旅遊的。

There will be one day that all participants are required to visit the local factory there together.
其中會有一天所有員工必須要一起參觀當地工廠。

For the rest of the time, a local tour guide will accompany us and make sure we all have a good time over there.
剩餘的時間會有當地導遊陪同我們旅遊，確保大家在當地都玩得開心。

(3) 聽寫（美國口音）

1. It is my great _____ to be here today.
   今天很榮幸來到這裡。

2. It's been more than one year since the _____ of two previous business entities.
   距離兩個業務單位合併，已經超過了一年。

3. Many of you have _____ many different opinions about this merge to me via e-mail.
   很多人都曾寫電子郵件給我，表達了對於合併各種不同的意見。

4. As Manager of Pacific Region, I believe the best way to communicate is to have open _____.

身為亞洲區經理，我認為公開對話是最佳的溝通方式。

track 123

5. That's why I few to Taipei to hold this meeting with you and to listen to your _____ personally.
這就是為什麼我飛到這裡來與你們開這個會，親自聆聽你們的想法。

6. Let's start with the new office where you two groups of people _____ share.
讓我們先從你們兩群員工現在共同分享的新辦公室開始討論。

7. Is there any _____ about the arrangement of working spaces?
對於這個工作空間的安排有人想說說意見嗎？

8. Of course, any _____ are welcome.
當然，任何其他的意見也可以提出來。

答案：

1. pleasure
2. integration
3. expressed
4. dialogues
5. concerns
6. currently

track 123

7. feedback

8. suggestions

(4) 跟讀（美國口音）

It is my great pleasure to be here today. It's been more than one year since the integration of the previous two business entities. Many of you have expressed many different opinions about this merge to me via e-mail. As Manager of Pacific Region, I believe the best way to communicate is to have open dialogues. That's why I few here to hold this meeting with you and to listen to your concerns personally. Let's start with the new office where you two groups of staff members currently share. Is there any feedback about the arrangement of working spaces? Of course, any other suggestions are welcome.

今天很榮幸來到這裡，距離兩個業務單位合併，已經超過了一年，很多人都曾寫電子郵件給我，表達了對於合併各種不同的意見。身為亞洲區經理，我認為公開對話是最佳的溝通方式，這就是為什麼我飛到這裡來與你們開這個會，親自聆聽你們的想法。讓我們先從你們兩群員工現在共同分享的新辦公室開始討論，對於這個工作空間的安排有人想說說意見嗎？當然，任何其他的意見也可以提出來。

track 124

(5) 常見片語與句型

常見片語	常見句型
address the meeting 在會上發言	**The chairperson is addressing the meeting.** 主席正在會上發言。
carry a motion 提議	**The motion is being carried by the manager.** 經理正在提議。
come to a conclusion 下結論	**By the end of today, we have to come to a conclusion.** 今天結束前，我們必須要得到結論。
deliver a presentation 做簡報	**It is not quite easy for him to deliver a presentation in English.** 對他來說，用英語做簡報不是件容易的事。
make a speech 發表演講	**Our CEO made a speech on the opening day of the factory.** 我們執行長在工廠開工日發表演講。
make an announcement 宣布	**The new director made an announcement to the public this afternoon.** 新主任今天下午對大眾宣布事項。
second a motion 附議	**We waited for somebody to second a motion but nobody did.** 我們等人來附議，但是沒有人。
take minutes 做會議記錄	**The secretary can take minutes very well.** 這位秘書可以將會議紀錄做得很好。
voting system 投票系統	**I do not fully understand the voting system of our company.** 我對我們公司的投票系統不甚了解。

Unit 7 人物介紹

　　人物介紹經常出現於典禮或正式宴會上，介紹了姓名後，通常會介紹現在所服務的公司，或是於哪類業界工作，有時也會包含學經歷，與哪些人熟識等等。

人物介紹例題

先解題

1. What is the purpose of the talk?

(A) To introduce a new person.

(B) To introduce a new system.

(C) To introduce a new design.

(D) To introduce a new office.

1. 這段談話的目的為何？

(A) 介紹新人。

(B) 介紹新系統。

(C) 介紹新設計。

(D) 介紹新辦公室。

正確答案：A

track 125

2. According to the speaker, why can all employees answer the intern's questions?

(A) There are not many questions.

(B) There are not many people.

track 125

(C) There is not much work.

(D) There is not much time.

2. 根據說話者，為什麼所有員工都可以回答實習生問題？

(A) 問題不多。

(B) 人數不多。

(C) 工作不多。

(D) 時間不多。

正確答案：B

3. What does "fit in" mean here?

(A) Stretch.

(B) Integrate.

(C) Understand.

(D) Locate.

3. 這裡的 **"fit in"** 是什麼意思？

(A) 拉扯。

(B) 融入。

(C) 了解。

(D) 定位。

正確答案：B

track 125

●獨白內文請見(4)跟讀

(1) 解析常見題目

大意

What is the short talk mainly about?
這段簡短談話的主題是什麼？

Who is the speaker introducing to the staff now?
發言者正在向員工介紹誰？

What job is the man going to do in the company?
這個男子將會在公司做什麼工作？

內容細節

Which department is the intern going to work in?
這個實習生將會在哪個部門工作？

When will the new employee start his new work?
這個新員工將在什麼時候開始新工作？

What can everyone consult the young man on?
大家可以向這個年輕人請問什麼事？

 track 126

(2) 常見句子

Good afternoon, may I introduce our guest, Mr. Baker, from the United States.

track 126

午安，我想向大家介紹我們的來賓，來自美國的貝克先生。

Mr. Baker used to work at our branch office in Chicago, and is now joining us in Taipei.
貝克先生曾經在我們芝加哥分公司工作過，現在他要來加入在台北的我們。

He has years of experiences in aromatherapy, which is a new area for our company.
他有多年芳香療法的經驗，這正是我們公司的新領域。

Kevin, could you please show Mr. Baker around the lab?
凱文，請你帶貝克先生參觀一下實驗室？

(3) 聽寫（加拿大口音）

1. Good morning, everyone, this is our new _____, Ted Anderson, who just finished MBA from University of Washington.
   大家早，這是我們的新實習生，泰德安德森，他剛由華盛頓大學取得了商業管理碩士。

2. He is going to work in the Sales _____ of our company for two months this summer.
   今年夏天將在我們的業務部門工作兩個月。

track 126

3. Since we are a small _____, all of you can answer his questions.
   既然我們是個小團隊，你們都可以回答他的問題。

4. He will _____ to Rachel directly though.
   不過他主要向瑞秋報告。

5. This young man is an expert in computer and has many software _____.
   這個年輕人是電腦高手，擁有很多軟體證書。

6. Please feel free to _____ him on IT issues.
   請盡量問他電腦資訊問題。

7. Hope he is going to _____ in immediately.
   希望他可以馬上融入我們。

答案：

    1. intern

    2. Department

    3. team

    4. report

    5. certificates

    6. consult

    7. fit

track 127

(4) 跟讀（加拿大口音）

Good morning, everyone, this is our new intern, Ted Anderson, who just finished MBA from University of Washington. He is going to work in the Sales Department of our company for two months this summer. Since we are a small team, all of you can answer his questions. He will report to Rachel directly though. This young man is an expert in computer and has many software certificates. Please feel free to consult him on IT issues. Hope he is going to fit in immediately.

大家早，這是我們的新實習生，泰德安德森，他剛由華盛頓大學取得了商業管理碩士，今年夏天將在我們的業務部門工作兩個月。既然我們是個小團隊，你們都可以回答他的問題，不過他主要向瑞秋報告，這個年輕人是電腦高手，擁有很多軟體證書，請盡量問他電腦問題。希望他可以馬上融入我們。

(5) 常見片語與句型

常見片語	常見句型
be a mentor 當導師	**It is not easy to be a mentor these days.** 現在要當導師不是件容易的事。
be senior/junior to 比……年長／年輕	**She is senior/junior to him by 3 years.** 她比他大 3 歲／小 3 歲。
become a leader 成為領導者	**After years of hard working, she became the leader of the department.** 經過好幾年辛苦工作後，她成為部門的領導者。
contribute to 貢獻	**Most of us want to contribute to the society.** 我們大多數人都想要對社會做出貢獻。
educational background 教育背景	**Please list your educational background in your resume.** 請在履歷表上列出你的教育背景。
gain experience 獲得經驗	**During this time, I gained experience in IT translation.** 在這段時間我獲得了資訊科技翻譯的經驗。
make introductions 介紹彼此認識	**Now everyone is here, let me start to make introductions.** 現在大家都在，讓我開始介紹彼此認識。
team up 合作	**To my surprise, we would team up with our competing company.** 讓我訝異的是，我們竟會與競爭對手合作。
trainee program 見習生計畫	**Many vocational schools have trainee programs with companies.** 很多職業學校與公司簽訂見習生計畫。

track 128

8 觀光導覽

　　觀光導覽於日常旅遊中經常出現，也常常運用於參訪公司與工廠的導覽，通常導覽員有固定的介紹內容順序，通常配合導覽地點的出現先後。

觀光導覽例題

先解題

1. What is most likely the speaker's job?

　(A) Care-giver.

　(B) Tourist guide.

　(C) Salesperson.

　(D) Manager.

1. 這位說話者的工作最可能為何？

　(A) 看護。

　(B) 導遊。

　(C) 業務員。

　(D) 經理。

正確答案：B

2. Why do the passengers have to get off the bus and walk?

　(A) The tourist bus is too huge to get in.

　(B) The car traffic is too bad in the zone.

(C) No people are allowed in the area.

(D) No cars can enter the zone.

2. 為什麼乘客必須要下巴士來走路？

(A) 觀光巴士太大，無法進入。

(B) 這地區的交通太糟糕。

(C) 這地區禁止人們入內。

(D) 這地區禁止車子入內。

正確答案：D

3. According to the speaker, what is considered best preserved in the Ximending area?

(A) Movie posters.

(B) Graffiti art.

(C) Pop music.

(D) Historic buildings.

3. 根據說話者，在西門町何者保存最佳？

(A) 電影海報。

(B) 塗鴉藝術。

(C) 流行音樂。

(D) 歷史建築。

正確答案：B

track 129

● 獨白內文請見 (4) 跟讀

(1) 解析常見題目

大意

What is the speaker showing around?
說話者在展示什麼？

Which tourist spot is the speaker talking about?
說話者在描述哪一個景點？

What kind of people are possibly the listeners?
聽眾可能是什麼樣的人？

內容細節

Where is the starting point of Ximending?
西門町的起點在哪裡？

What is best-preserved in Ximending?
西門町保存最好的是什麼？

Who are the most likely fans of Ximending?
誰最有可能熱愛西門町？

What is probably the speaker's job?
說話者可能從事什麼工作？

track 129

(2) 常見句子

Welcome to the Taipei Botanic Garden, and I'm here to answer all the questions you might have.
歡迎來到台北植物園，很高興能在這裡回答您任何的問題。

The plants with the Botanic Garden change with each season and the landscape accordingly.
這個植物園的植物隨著季節和景觀而改變。

This is the Lotus Pond, where many people like to take photos or do painting around.
這個就是很多人喜歡攝影或寫生的荷花池。

Over there is the National Museum of History, where excellent exhibitions are frequently held.
那邊就是歷史博物館，經常有舉辦精彩的展覽。

(3) 聽寫（英國口音）

1. Ladies and Gentlemen, welcome to the Taipei _____ deck tourist bus.
   各位女士先生，歡迎來到台北觀光雙層巴士。

2. On your right side, you can see the MRT Exit 6, which is the _____ of Ximending.
   在您的右手邊是捷運 6 號，也就是西門町的起點。

track 130

3. A bit further, on your left side, you see the Red Build-ing, which used to _____ as movie theaters.
再過去一點，在您的左手邊是紅樓，曾經是電影院。

4. Let's get off the tourist bus now and take a _____ walk.
現在我們下觀光巴士，隨意逛一逛。

5. As you can see, Ximending is a _____ zone completely.
你們應看得出來，西門町完全是個徒步區。

6. The shops along offer _____ items of pop culture, and street performers are almost everywhere.
周圍這些店家提供年輕人的流行商品，到處可見街頭藝人。

7. Now we've come to this area, where huge _____ can be seen on many walls.
現在我們來到這個地區，很多牆上可以看見大幅塗鴉。

8. This is considered the best-preserved Street Art in Taiwan, and it consistently _____.
這算是台灣保存最好的街頭藝術，而且不斷在更新。

答案：

1. double
2. start
3. serve
4. leisure
5. pedestrian
6. trendy
7. graffiti
8. updates

(4) 跟讀（英國口音）

Ladies and Gentlemen, welcome to the Taipei double deck tourist bus. On your right side, you can see the MRT Exit 6, which is the start of Ximending. A bit further, on your left side, you see the Red Building, which used to serve as movie theaters. Let's get off the tourist bus now and take a leisure walk. As you can see, Ximending is a pedestrian zone completely. The shops along offer trendy items of pop culture, and street performers are almost everywhere.

Now we've come to this area, where huge graffiti can be seen on many walls. This is considered the best-preserved Street Art in Taiwan, and it consistently updates.

track 131

　　各位女士先生，歡迎來到台北觀光商雙層巴士，在您的右手邊是捷運 6 號，也就是西門町的起點，再過去一點，在您的左手邊是紅樓，曾經是電影院。現在我們下觀光巴士，隨意逛一逛，你們應該看得出來，西門町完全是個徒步區，周圍這些店家提供年輕人的流行商品，到處可見街頭藝人。現在我們來到這個地區，很多牆上可以看見大幅塗鴉，這算是台灣保存最好的街頭藝術，而且不斷在更新。

(5) 常見片語與句型

常見片語	常見句型
Bed & Breakfast 民宿	**The business of Bed & Breakfasts suffers much during the pandemic.** 疫情期間民宿業受到很大衝擊。
collect souvenirs 收集紀念品	**Many travelers like to collect souvenirs of places they have visited.** 很多遊客喜歡收集所到之地的紀念品。
do sightseeing 觀光	**There are many ways to do sightseeing without damaging the local ecology.** 有很多不會傷害到當地生態的觀光方式。
flora and fauna 珍禽奇獸；奇花異草	**The flora and fauna of Australia is very unique.** 澳大利亞的自然生態非常獨特。

track 131

local history 當地歷史	Good tour guides can explain the local history very well. 好的導遊可以將當地歷史解釋得很好。
pedestrian zone 徒步區	It would be safer to walk in pedestrian zones than in other places. 在徒步區行走比在其它地方來得安全。
scenic spot 風景區	This is a scenic spot you must see during this tour in this country. 這裡是來此國的必訪景點。
summer getaway 夏天旅遊去處	This tropical island is a summer getaway for people from cold areas. 這個熱帶島嶼是來自寒冷地區的人們的夏天旅遊去處。
tour guide 導遊	Quite a few tour guides know several foreign languages. 相當多的導遊通曉數國語言。

Unit 9 活動解說

　　活動解說強調的是活動流程的解釋，內容多為實務的分解步驟，因此只要掌握了活動主題，程序通常就會按照先後順序出現，不會有任何問題。

活動解說例題

先解題

1. What is the general topic of the talk?

(A) Preparing a singing competition.

(B) Preparing a birthday party.

(C) Preparing a birthday gift.

(D) Preparing a farewell dinner.

1. 這段談話的大意為何？

(A) 準備一場歌唱比賽。

(B) 準備一場生日慶祝會。

(C) 準備一個生日禮物。

(D) 準備一場歡送會。

正確答案：D

2. What are the listeners asked to do?

(A) To present the birthday gift.

(B) To write down their thoughts.

track 132

(C) To come up with a gift idea.

(D) To design a digital e-card.

2. 聽眾被要求做什麼？

(A) 拿出生日禮物。

(B) 寫下他們的感想。

(C) 提出禮物點子。

(D) 設計數位電子賀卡。

正確答案：B

3. What is most likely the relationship between the listeners and Mr. Chen?

(A) Coworkers.

(B) Clients.

(C) Partners.

(D) Bosses.

3. 聽眾和陳先生最可能是什麼關係？

(A) 同事。

(B) 客戶。

(C) 夥伴。

(D) 老闆。

正確答案：A

track 133

● 獨白內文請見(4)跟讀

(1) 解析常見題目

大意

What is the party this Friday for?
這星期五的聚會目的是什麼？

What is planned on the farewell party?
這個歡送會計畫有什麼活動？

How is the party going to be proceeded?
這個聚會的流程是怎麼樣的？

內容細節

What is Mr. Chen going to do after his retirement?
陳先生退休後要做什麼？

What will be presented to Mr. Chen?
陳先生會收到什麼？

When will the surprise gift and card be given to Mr. Chen?
陳先生什麼時候會收到驚奇禮物和卡片？

Who are mostly going to attend this party?
誰最可能參加這個聚會？

track 133

(2) 常見句子

Hi everyone, welcome to the yearly charity concert of our company at the basement A12.

大家好，歡迎來到位於地下室A12 的公司年度慈善音樂會。

This evening our sales Manager, Peter, will play the piano, and our secretary, Amy, will play the flute.

今晚我們的業務經理彼得會為我們表演鋼琴，秘書艾美會表演長笛。

We hope you enjoy the duo performance prepared by our colleagues.

我們希望大家會喜歡我們同事準備的雙重奏。

Please donate the money to the piggy bank, and we will use the money to help the homeless people here.

請在小豬撲滿內放下捐款，我們會用這些錢來幫助這裡的街友。

track 134

(3) 聽寫（美國口音）

1. This Friday evening, there is going to be a _____ party for our Mr. Chen.

   這個星期五晚上將會有場為我們的陳先生舉辦的歡送會。

track 134

2. He is going to _____ from our company and to start his own charity work.
他將從我們公司退休，開始自己的慈善工作。

3. As his colleagues, we've prepared a _____ microphone to give Mr. Chen because he likes to sing so much.
身為他的同事，我們準備了一個數位麥克風要送給陳先生，因為他是如此熱愛唱歌。

4. Please write down your _____ words for him on this big card.
請於這張大賀卡上寫下你們的感言。

5. I'm sure you've got much to say to him after years of working _____.
我想你們在一起工作這麼多年，一定會有很多想說的話。

6. Shane will present the card and the gift to Mr. Chen after the _____ is made at the dining table. Thank you.
玄恩會於餐桌敬酒後將卡片與禮物交給陳先生。謝謝大家。

答案：

　1. farewell

　2. retire

3. digital

4. thoughtful

5. together

6. toast

(4) 跟讀（美國口音）

This Friday evening, there is going to be a farewell party for our Mr. Chen. He is going to retire from our company and to start his own charity work. As his colleagues, we've prepared a digital microphone to give Mr. Chen because he likes to sing so much. Please write down your thoughtful words for him on this big card. I'm sure you've got much to say to him after years of working together. Shane will present the card and the gift to Mr. Chen after the toast is made at the dining table. Thank you.

這個星期五晚上將會有場為我們的陳先生舉辦的歡送會，他將從我們公司退休，開始自己的慈善工作，身為他的同事，我們準備了一個數位麥克風要送給陳先生，因為他是如此熱愛唱歌。請於這張大賀卡上寫下你們的感言，我想你們在一起工作這麼多年，一定會有很多想說的話，玄恩會於餐桌敬酒後將卡片與禮物交給陳先生。謝謝大家。

track 135

(5) 常見片語與句型

常見片語	常見句型
casual vibe 輕鬆氛圍	We could feel a casual vibe at the farewell party. 我們可以感受到歡送會的輕鬆氛圍。
charity event 慈善活動	Our company always have charity events during the end of the year. 我們公司於歲末年終都會舉辦慈善活動。
donate funds 捐款	The head of the foundation donated funds to several universities. 基金會董事長捐了款給幾所大學。
event host/hostess 活動主持人／女主持人	The event hostess of the music award is Lady Gaga. 音樂頒獎典禮的主持人是女神卡卡。
event manager 活動策劃人	The event manager did a good job in organizing this ceremony. 活動策劃人將這個典禮安排得很好。
give a reception to 給某人辦歡迎會	They gave a warm reception to the newcomer to the company. 他們給了公司新成員辦了一個歡迎會。
give the rundown 提供流程表	The host gave the rundown of the wedding reception. 主持人提供了婚禮的流程表。
set the tone for 為……定調	The soft music set the tone for the workshop for trainees. 溫柔的音樂為實習生工作坊定了調。
special effect 特殊效果	The special effects can help the people with disabilities experience computer games. 這些特殊效果能幫助身障人士體驗電腦遊戲。
visual aid 視覺輔助	Viewers can benefit much from the visual aids of the statistics. 統計數字的視覺輔助非常有助於理解。

track 135

U n i t
10 講解流程

　　流程解說強調的是機器操作流程的解釋，例如販賣機的使用分解步驟，內容一定會按照先後順序出現，只要專心聽即可。

講解流程例題

　　Attention, Wilson's shoppers. We will be explaining to you how our new machine of fresh orange juice works. First, insert the cash or coins and then press the bottom after enough money is paid. At this point, you can see the orange being squeezed by the machine and the fresh orange juice made in front of you. Open the lid and take out the cup of orange juice. The extra change will come out of the machine instantly for you to retrieve. All this is done in less than 3 minutes automatically in front of your eyes, and this is the wonder of the orange machine. Thank you for your attention.

　　威爾森顧客請注意，我們將會為您解釋這台新型自動榨柳橙機如何運作，首先投入鈔票或銅板，投夠錢後按這個鈕，這時您可以看見機器現場榨柳橙，柳橙汁會在您面前榨好，打開這個蓋子，就可以拿到這杯柳橙汁，找錢會自動掉出機器讓您自取，這些都在 3 分鐘內自動在您眼前做完，這就是這台機器奇妙之處。謝謝大家。

track 136

(1)

● **Put in cash or coins**
　放入鈔票或硬幣

(2)

● **Press the bottom**
　按按鈕

(3)

● **Orange juice is being squeezed**
　柳橙汁正在榨

(4)

● **Open the lid & take out the product**
　打開蓋子，取出產品

(5)

● **Take the extra change**
　找錢自取

先解題

1. What is the topic of the short talk?

(A) Talking about the origins of the fresh fruit.

(B) Announcing the special discounts of the orange juice.

(C) Demonstrating how the new orange machine works.

(D) Showing how the orange cake is made automatically.

1. 這段談話的主題是什麼？

(A) 談論新鮮水果的來源地。

(B) 公佈柳橙汁的特別折扣。

(C) 展示新柳橙機器運作過程。

(D) 展示柳橙蛋糕自動製作過程。

正確答案：C

2. What is the speaker probably doing while giving the talk?

(A) Showing how the machine works.

(B) Counting the coins to be inserted.

(C) Choosing the size of the product.

(D) Putting the fresh fruit in the machine.

track 136

2. 這位說話者可能一邊談話，一邊在做什麼？

(A) 展示機器如何運作。

(B) 數著要塞入的銅板。

(C) 選擇產品的尺寸。

(D) 將新鮮水果放入機器。

正確答案：A

 track 137

3. According to the speaker, when can the customer retrieve the extra coins?

(A) Before getting the orange juice.

(B) At the same time of making the orange juice.

(C) As soon as paying the money.

(D) After taking out the orange juice.

3. 根據說話者，什麼時候消費者可以取回多餘的銅板？

(A) 在取出柳橙汁前。

(B) 在製作柳橙汁的同時。

(C) 付錢後馬上就可以。

(D) 在取出柳橙汁後。

正確答案：D

● 獨白內文請見(4)跟讀

(1) 解析常見題目

大意

What is the subject of this short talk?
這段簡短談話的主題為何？

What is the man explaining?
這個男子在解釋什麼？

What is the man's short talk about?
這個男子的簡短談話是關於什麼？

內容細節

What is the salesperson demonstrating?
這個業務員正在展示什麼？

What is the special feature of such a machine?
這個機器的特點是什麼？

What can be seen in front of the customers?
顧客可以看見什麼展示於眼前？

Why can this automatic machine save man power?
為什麼這個自動機器可以節省人力？

track 138

(2) 常見句子

Attention everyone. Please line up to take the Maokong Gondola from the Taipei Zoo.
大家好，請要搭乘貓纜到貓空的乘客排好隊。

The one-way price is 120 NTD, but for Taipei residents, special discount, 50 NTD.
單程車資120元，但是台北市市民優惠價50元。

For children and the people with disabilities, the special one-way price is 50 NTD, too.
小孩和身心障礙人士單程優惠價也是50元。

There are special crystal cabins, where you can see the tea fields directly under the floor of the cabin.
搭乘特別水晶纜車可以直接看見纜車地板下方的茶園。

Many people choose to take the Maokong Gondola for the return trip as well.
很多人選擇回程也搭乘貓纜。

(3) 聽寫（英國口音）

1. Attention, Wilson's shoppers. We will be _____ to you how our new machine of fresh orange juice works.
威爾森顧客請注意，我們將會為您解釋這台新型自動榨柳橙機如何運作。

track 138

2. First, _____ the cash or coins and then press the bottom after enough money is paid.
   首先投入鈔票或銅板，投夠錢後按這個鈕。

3. At this point, you can see the orange being _____ by the machine and the fresh orange juice being made in front of you.
   這時您可以看見機器現場榨柳橙，柳橙汁在您面前榨好。

4. Open the _____ and take out the cup of orange juice.
   打開這個蓋子，就可以拿到這杯柳橙汁。

5. The extra change will come out of the machine instantly for you to _____ .
   找錢會自動掉出機器讓您自取。

6. All this is done in less than 3 minutes _____ in front of your eyes, and this is the wonder of the orange machine.
   這些都在 3 分鐘內自動在您眼前做完，這就是這台機器奇妙之處。

7. Thank you for your _____ .
   謝謝大家。

- -

答案：

   1. explaining

   2. insert

   3. squeezed

4. lid

5. retrieve

6. automatically

7. attention

 track 139

(4) 跟讀（英國口音）

講解流程

Attention, Wilson's shoppers. We will be explaining to you how our new machine of fresh orange juice works. First, insert the cash or coins and then press the bottom after enough money is paid. At this point, you can see the orange being squeezed by the machine and the fresh orange juice being made in front of you. Open the lid and take out the cup of orange juice. The extra change will come out of the machine instantly for you to retrieve. All this is done in less than 3 minutes automatically in front of your eyes, and this is the wonder of the orange machine. Thank you for your attention.

威爾森顧客請注意，我們將會為您解釋這台新型自動榨柳橙機如何運作，首先投入鈔票或銅板，投夠錢後按這個鈕，這時您可以看見機器現場榨柳橙，柳橙汁會在您面前榨好，打開這個蓋子，就可以拿到這杯柳橙汁，找錢會自動掉出機器讓您自取，這些都在 3 分鐘內自動在您眼前做完，這就是這台機器奇妙之處。謝謝大家。

(5) 常見片語與句型

常見片語	常見句型
adopt methods 採用方式	We should adopt new methods of educating our new staff. 我們應該要採用新方法來教育新員工。
break down 分解	If you break down the process, you will find it not hard at all. 如果你將這過程分解為幾個步驟，就一點也不會覺得難了。
carry out the instructions 照指示做	The personal assistant carried out the manger's instructions. 這位助理按照經理的指示進行工作。
follow the direction 按照指示	You cannot go wrong if you follow the direction carefully. 只要你仔細按照指示，絕對不會出錯。
make demolition 拆毀	Before making demolition, you have to get the owner's approval. 在拆毀房屋前你一定要得到屋主的同意。
SOP = Standard Operating Procedure 標準作業程序	Checking references before we do business with an agent is our standard operating procedure. 與代理商往來前，要先查核背景是我們的標準作業程序。
step by step 按部就班	Please follow the SOP and do it step by step. 請按照標準作業程序按步就班來進行。

track 140

● 開始做些初階的題目吧

照片描述

解說：在這個部分的每一題，你都會聽到四個關於一張照片的描述，當你聽到這些描述時，必須要選出一個對你所看到照片的最佳描述，然後在答案紙上相對應的題號下劃記作答，這些描述不會在你的測驗本上印出來，而且只會播放一次。

1. **Look at the picture marked number 1 on your test book.**

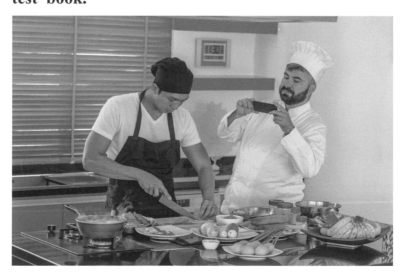

track 140

(A) One of the men is watching a cooking show.

(B) One of the men is cutting an ingredient.

(C) One of the men is shouting at the other guy.

(D) One of the men is frying chicken.

請看試題冊上的第 1 題的這張照片。

(A) 其中一個男子正在看烹飪節目。

(B) 其中一個男子正在切食材。

(C) 其中一個男子正在對另一個男子大吼。

(D) 其中一個男子正在煎雞肉。

正確選項：B

track 141

2. Look at the picture marked number 2 on your test book.

track 141

(A) The woman is doing an online shopping.

(B) The woman is making a schedule for her boss.

(C) The woman is browsing on the Internet.

(D) The woman is doing a teleconferencing.

請看試題冊上的第2題的這張照片。

(A) 這位女子正在網購。

(B) 這位女子正在為她的老闆排時程表。

(C) 這位女子正在瀏覽網路。

(D) 這位女子正在開視訊會議。

正確選項：D

3. Look at the picture marked number 3 on your test book.

(A) The woman seems to be very upset.

(B) The woman is talking to somebody on the phone.

(C) The woman is working overtime.

(D) The woman is reporting to her boss.

請看試題冊上的第3題的這張照片。

(A) 這位女子看起來很沮喪。

(B) 這位女子正在電話與人通話中。

(C) 這位女子正在加班。

(D) 這位女子正在向她老闆作報告。

正確選項：B

 track 142

4. **Look at the picture marked number 4 on your test book.**

track 142

(A) There are many tourists on the beach.

(B) This place is very suitable for surfing.

(C) There is a small boat on the shore.

(D) Many people are enjoying water sport here.

請看試題冊上的第4題的這張照片。

(A) 海灘上有很多觀光客。

(B) 這地方很適合衝浪。

(C) 海岸邊有一艘小船。

(D) 很多人正在這裡享受水上運動。

正確選項：C

2 應答問題

你會聽到一個用英語表達的問題或陳述，還有三個回答，這些都不會印在測驗本上，而且只播放一次，請選出對於此問題或陳述的最佳反應，然後在答案紙上劃記(A) 或 (B) 或 (C)。

1. (W-Br): You wouldn't have time to check the report for me, would you?

(M-Am): (A) You can report to me.

(B) You wouldn't tell me.

(C) I think I can make time for it.

1.（女－英）：你不會有時間為我檢查報告，對吧？

（男－美）：(A)妳可以向我報告。

(B)妳不肯告訴我。

(C)我想我可以挪出時間來。

正確選項：C

2. (M-Aus): Why don't you ask Ms. Lin yourself?

(W-Am): (A) Because I don't know.

(B) I don't think she would tell me.

(C) She can take care of herself.

2.（男－澳）：妳為什麼不自己去問林小姐？

（女－美）：(A)因為我不知道。

(B)我覺得她不會告訴我。

(C)她可以照顧自己。

正確選項：B

3. (W-Br): Where did you hear the news?

(M-Am): (A) When I walked past the office.

(B) I read it on the Internet.

(C) It is not my fault.

3. （女－英）：你在哪裡聽到這個消息的？

（男－美）：(A)當我經過郵局時。

(B)我在網路上看到的。

(C)這不是我的錯。

正確選項：B

 track 143

4. **(M-Am): What's wrong with the fax machine?**

(W-Aus): (A) There is a paper jam in the fax machine.

(B) Yes, it is my turn.

(C) No, I don't mind.

4. （男－美）：傳真機出了什麼問題？

（女－澳）：(A)傳真機卡紙了。

(B)是的，輪到我了。

(C)不，我不介意。

正確選項：A

5. **(W-Br): How often do you visit your parents?**

(M-Am): (A) One and half hours.

(B) Once a month.

(C) I often work overtime.

5. （女－英）：你多久去看你父母一次？

（男－美）：(A)一個小時半。

(B)一個月一次。

(C)我經常加班。

track 143

正確選項：B

6. **(M-Cn): This must be fake news.**

 (W-Aus): (A) We bought the newspaper.

     (B) You'll have to fake it.

     (C) How can you be so sure?

6. （男－加）：這一定是假新聞。

 （女－澳）：(A)報紙是我們買的。

     (B)你得要假裝一下。

     (C)你怎麼能這麼確定？

正確選項：C

 track 144

Part 3 簡短對話

 解說：你會聽到兩人或多人之間的對話，你必須要回答關於每段對話的三個問題，請選出每個問題的最佳答案，然後在答案紙上劃記(A) 或 (B) 或 (C)或 (D)，這些對話不會在你的測驗本上印出來，而且只會播放一次。

track 144

(M-Am): What do you think of exporting medicinal alcohol to the UK during the pandemic time?

(W-Aus): That sounds like a good idea, but I'm not sure if our government controls the export medicinal alcohol now.

(M-Am): Besides, we'll have to find out how new Brexit trading rules apply to this.

(W-Aus): Thank you for reminding us of it.

(M-Am): I'll look it up on the Internet.

(W-Aus): Keep me in the loop.

1. What is the topic of their conversation?

(A) When to export alcoholic drinks to the UK.

(B) How to export an item to the UK.

(C) Brexit and Europe.

(D) How to do business with Europe.

2. What does the woman think of the idea the man brought up?

(A) She does not think it would work.

(B) She does not like to do business with Britain.

(C) She does not have any experiences doing business with the UK.

(D) She does not know if the item is of free trading.

3. What does the woman mean by "Keep me in the loop"?

(A) Keep me profitable after Brexit.

(B) Keep me stable during this time.

(C) Keep me informed about it.

(D) Keep me in control of the expenses.

（男－美）：你覺得在這個疫情期間對英國出口藥用酒精怎麼樣？

（女－澳）：這個主意聽來不錯，但是我不確定現在我們政府是否管制藥用酒精出口。

（男－美）：除此以外，我們必須查一下英國脫歐後相關的新貿易規定。

（女－澳）：謝謝提醒我們這一點。

（男－美）：我來上網搜尋這事。

（女－澳）：讓我隨時得知最新進展。

1. 這段對話的主題是什麼？

(A)什麼時候向英國出口酒精飲品。

(B)如何向英國出口某項貨品。

(C)英國脫歐與歐洲。

(D)如何與歐洲做生意。

正確選項：B

2. 這位女士覺得男子提出的主意怎麼樣？

(A)她不認為會成功。

(B)她不喜歡跟英國做生意。

(C)她不曾跟英國做過生意。

(D)她不確定這項貨品是否可以自由交易。

正確選項：D

3. 這位女士說 "**keep me in the loop**" 是什麼意思？

(A)讓我在英國脫歐後有利可圖。

(B)讓我在這個時期保持穩定。

(C)讓我隨時得知最新進展。

(D)讓我掌管費用支出。

正確選項：C

track 145

簡短獨白

解說：你會聽到幾段一個人的獨白，你必須要回答關於每段獨白的三個問題，請選出每個問題的最佳答案，然後在答案紙上劃記(A) 或 (B) 或(C)或 (D)，這些獨白不會在測驗本上印出來，而且只會播放一次。

track 145

Due to the pandemic, our school has adopted remote learning, mostly online learning. Recently we conducted a survey among the teachers of several subjects, and the result of some average satisfaction rates is as below.

Subjects	Average satisfaction rate among teachers
English	83%
Chinese	77%
Math	63%
Physical Education	51%
Music	57%

As we can see, both English and Chinese teachers find the effects of online teaching satisfactory, which they partly give credit to the software applications they use. Music and Physical Education teachers do not seem to appreciate online instruction that much since the nature of their courses requires students' active practice.

Even though many teachers and students look forward to face-to-face contacts with each other, it is believed that distance education will prevail for a while. All in all, in the future we encourage more engagement and interaction online from teachers and students.

track 146

1. **What is the general subject of this talk?**

   (A) The pandemic and the economics.

   (B) The evaluation of online teaching and learning.

   (C) The plan for school reopening.

   (D) The subjects school children learn.

2. **According to the table, teachers of which subject think most highly of online teaching?**

   (A) Chinese.

   (B) Physical Education.

   (C) English.

   (D) Music.

3. **What is expected with online learning by the speaker of this talk?**

   (A) The teachers and students get more involved in online courses.

   (B) The teachers adopt better software applications.

   (C) The students practice more than the teachers.

   (D) The teachers test their students more often than before.

因為疫情我們學校已經採用遠距教學，主要以線上教學為主。最近我們對幾個科目的老師進行了問卷調查，平均滿意率結果如以下所示。

track 146

科目	老師的平均滿意率
英文	**83%**
國文	**77%**
數學	**63%**
體育	**51%**
音樂	**57%**

　　我們可以看到，英文和國文老師都對於線上教學成果感到滿意，他們將部分原因歸功於所使用的應用軟體，音樂和體育老師似乎對線上教學不甚滿意，因為他們的課程本質上需要靠學生主動練習。

　　雖然很多老師與學生期待彼此面對面的接觸，一般認為遠距教學會持續盛行好一陣子。總體來說，我們鼓勵老師和學生有更多的線上參與和互動。

1. 這段談話的主題是什麼？
(A) 疫情和經濟。
(B) 線上教學的評量。
(C) 學校復學的計畫。
(D) 學齡兒童的學習科目。

track 146

正確選項：B

2. 根據這個表格，哪個科目的老師對線上教學最滿意？

　(A) 國文。

　(B) 體育。

　(C) 英文。

　(D) 音樂。

正確選項：C

3. 這段談話的說話者期待什麼？

　(A) 老師和學生對線上課程有更多參與。

　(B) 老師使用更好的應用軟體。

　(C) 學生比老師多練習。

　(D) 老師比從前更常測驗學生。

　　正確選項：A

New TOEIC
New TOEIC

5

聽力模擬試題

track 147

一回模擬試題

Part 1 照片描述

Directions : For each question in this part, you will hear four statements about a picture in your test book. When you hear the statements, you must select the one statement that best describes what you see in the picture. Then find the number of the question on your answer sheet and mark your answer. The statements will not be printed in your test book and will be spoken only one time.

解說：在這個部分的每一題，你都會聽到四個關於一張照片的描述，當你聽到這些描述時，必須要選出一個對你所看到照片的最佳描述，然後在答案紙上相對應的題號下劃記作答，這些描述不會在你的測驗本上印出來，而且只會播放一次。

track 147

1. **Look at the picture marked number one on your test book.**

   (A) They are playing table tennis.

   (B) They are playing a computer game.

   (C) They are playing tennis outdoors.

   (D) They are playing badminton

請看試題冊上的第 1 題的這張照片。

(A) 他們在打桌球。

(B) 他們在打電玩。

(C) 他們在戶外打網球。

(D) 他們在戶外打羽毛球。

track 148

2. **Look at the picture marked number two on your test book.**

(A) Many people are standing in a line to enter the shop.

(B) It is a bakery shop with cakes and bread.

(C) A clerk is serving the customers.

(D) Many customers are buying coffee here.

請看試題冊上的第 2 題的這張照片。

(A) 很多人正排隊等著進入店家。

(B) 這是家賣蛋糕與麵包的烘焙坊。

(C) 一個店員正在服務客人。

(D) 很多人正在這裡買咖啡。

track 148

3. **Look at the picture marked number three on your test book.**

(A) A man is playing the guitar while standing.

(B) A woman is playing the flute.

(C) A man is playing the guitar while sitting.

(D) A woman is singing while sitting.

請看試題冊上的第 3 題的這張照片。

(A) 一男子正站著彈吉他。

(B) 一女子正在吹長笛。

(C) 一男子正坐著彈吉他。

(D) 一女子正坐著唱歌。

track 149

4. Look at the picture marked number four on your test book.

(A) They are having an argument.

(B) They are listening to a presentation.

(C) They are listening to a lecture.

(D) They are having a friendly discussion.

請看試題冊上的第 4 題的這張照片。

(A) 他們正在爭論。

(B) 他們正在聽簡報。

(C) 他們正在聽講座。

(D) 他們正在愉快地討論著。

track 149

5. **Look at the picture marked number five on your test book.**

(A) It looks like a city full of tall buildings.

(B) It seems to be an area full of factories.

(C) It looks like a village at sunrise.

(D) It seems to be a farmland with cows.

請看試題冊上的第 5 題的這張照片。

(A) 看起來這是座有很多高樓的城市。

(B) 看起來這是個有很多工廠的地區。

(C) 看起來這是個黎明時的村莊。

(D) 看起來這是個有很多牛的農地。

5 聽力模擬試題

 track 150

6. **Look at the picture marked number six on your test book.**

(A) Two people are taking a walk together.

(B) Two people are cleaning the street.

(C) Two people are having a chat.

(D) Two people are feeding birds.

請看試題冊上的第 6 題的這張照片。

(A) 兩個人正在散步。

(B) 兩個人正在清理街道。

(C) 兩個人正在聊天。

(D) 兩個人正在餵鳥。

2 應答問題

Directions : You will hear a question or statement and three responses spoken in English. They will not be printed in your test book and will be spoken only one time. Select the best response to the question or statement and mark the letter (A), (B), or (C) on your answer sheet.

解說：你會聽到一個用英語表達的問題或陳述，還有三個回答，這些都不會印在測驗本上，而且只播放一次，請選出對於此問題或陳述的最佳反應，然後在答案紙上劃記 (A) 或 (B) 或 (C)。

符號註解：

Am＝美國
Cn＝加拿大
Br＝英國
Aus＝澳洲

track 151

7. (M-Am): Hello, who is speaking?

(W-Br): (A) This is Julia speaking.

(B) When will he call?

(C) I'll call you back.

7.（男－美）：請問您是哪位？

（女－英）：(A) 我是茱莉亞。

(B) 他何時會回電？

(C) 我會回您電話。

8. (W-Aus): What should I wear to the party?

(M-Cn): (A) Your outfit is out of style.

(B) I like your blouse.

(C) Anything you like.

8.（女－澳）：我該穿什麼出席宴會？

（男－加）：(A) 妳的穿著已過時。

(B) 我很喜歡妳的短衫。

(C) 任何妳想穿的都可以。

9. (M-Am): Don't you think your plan is not realistic?

(W-Aus): (A) It is not about the future.

(B) What makes you think so?

(C) I'd like to travel in the United States.

9.（男－美）：妳不覺得妳的計畫不切實際嗎？

（女－澳）：(A) 這與未來無關。

(B) 為什麼你會這麼想？

(C) 我想要到美國一遊。

track 151

10. (W-Br): Sorry for being late again.

(M-Cn): (A) It's okay.

(B) Thank you very much.

(C) When did it happen?

10.（女－英）：抱歉我遲到了。

（男－加）：(A) 沒關係。

(B) 非常謝謝妳。

(C) 這是什麼時候發生的？

11. (M-Br): Would you like to have dinner with me tonight?

(W-Am): (A) I'll keep the secret.

(B) Don't mention it.

(C) I'd love to.

11.（男－英）：今晚妳想要與我一起共進晚餐嗎？

（女－美）：(A) 我會保密。

(B) 沒關係。

(C) 非常樂意。

12. (M-Am): Have you been to Kyoto?

(W-Aus): (A) In a hotel near the city.

(B) Both for business and for sightseeing.

(C) No, but I'd like to go.

12.（男－美）：妳去過京都嗎？

（女－澳）：(A) 在靠近市區的飯店。

(B) 為了工作，也為了觀光。

(C) 沒去過，但是我想去。

 track 152

13. (W-Br): Don't you know our CEO from the US is coming in two days?

(M-Am): (A) I'll go on a business trip to the US.

(B) Our CFO is from the US.

(C) Of course.

13. （女－英）：你不知道我們的美籍執行長過兩天會來嗎？

（男－美）：(A) 我會去美國出差。

(B) 我們的財務長是從美國人。

(C) 當然知道。

14. (M-Aus): May I smoke here?

(W-Am): (A) Not really.

(B) I quit smoking.

(C) Tobacco costs a lot.

14. （男－澳）：我可以抽菸嗎？

（女－美）：(A) 不可以。

(B) 我戒菸了。

(C) 菸很貴。

15. (W-Am): How did you send the products to the clients?

(M-Br): (A) Ten days ago.

(B) By Airmail.

(C) Via e-mails.

15.（女－美）：你如何寄產品給客戶？

（男－英）：(A) 10 天前。

(B) 用航空郵寄。

(C) 透過電子郵件。

16. (M-Aus): You haven't seen that young man, have you?

(W-Cn): (A) No, not much.

(B) No, as far as I can remember.

(C) Yes, it depends.

16.（男－澳）：妳沒有見過那個年輕男子吧？

（女－加）：(A) 沒有，並不多。

(B) 沒有，就我所知沒有。

(C) 是的，不一定。

17. (M-Am): Which university did you go to?

(W-Aus): (A) I didn't attend any college.

(B) Which one would you like?

(C) Anyone will do.

17.（男－美）：你是讀哪個大學的？

（女－澳）：(A) 我沒有上大學。

(B) 你喜歡哪一個？

(C) 任何一個都好。

track 153

18. (W-Br): Do you know what green business is?

(M-Am): (A) Never been there before.

(B) Green vegetables are popular.

(C) Something like organic farming.

18.（女－英）：你知道什麼是綠事業嗎？

（男－美）：(A) 從未到過那裡。

(B) 綠色植物很流行。

(C) 像是有機耕種。

19. (M-Cn): I haven't tried to learn Greek.

(W-Aus): (A) I wouldn't try it.

(B) Take it easy.

(C) Greek myths are fascinating.

19.（男－加）：我沒有嘗試過學希臘文。

（女－澳）：(A) 我不會嘗試學。

(B) 放輕鬆點。

(C) 希臘神話很迷人。

20. (W-Br): Why didn't you raise the proposal in the meeting?

(M-Am): (A) I just got a raise in salary.

(B) Did you propose to your girlfriend?

(C) I'll let you do that.

20.（女－英）：你為什麼不在會議上提出這個提案？

（男－美）：(A) 我剛得到加薪。

(B) 你跟你女友求婚了嗎？

(C) 我讓你來提案。

21. (M-Aus): I heard he was fired yesterday.

(W-Cn): (A) Didn't he quit?

(B) It wasn't my day yesterday.

(C) Whatever will do.

21.（男－澳）：我聽說他昨天被開除了。

（女－加）：(A) 他不是辭職了嗎？

(B) 昨天我一切不順。

(C) 什麼都可以。

22. (W-Am): How do you like our new colleague?

(M-Br): (A) He is an IT expert.

(B) He is from the United States.

(C) He seems to be a nice person.

22.（女－美）：你覺得我們新來的同事如何？

（男－英）：(A) 他是一位資訊科技專家。

(B) 他來自美國。

(C) 他似乎人不錯。

23. (W-Br): Isn't the yearly performance self-evaluation due on December 10?

(M-Cn): (A) Everyone should do it online.

(B) Yes, it's moved to December 17.

(C) Yes, I've already finished it and sent it online.

track 153

23.（女－英）：年度表現自我評估不是**12**月**10**日要
交？

（男－加）：(A) 每個人都要在線上填寫。

(B) 是的，已經延到12月17日。

(C) 是的，我已經在線上完成並寄出。

 track 154

24. (M-Am): Who should I report the case to?

(W-Br): (A) Take care of yourself.

(B) You have to.

(C) You can talk to me.

24.（男－美）：我該向誰報告這案子？

（女－英）：(A) 請保重。

(B) 你必須要。

(C) 你可以跟我說。

25. (W-Aus): How many colleagues are there in your office?

(M-Cn): (A) About a dozen.

(B) They haven't arrived.

(C) Whenever they like.

25.（女－澳）：你辦公室有幾個同事？

（男－加）：(A) 大概 12 人。

(B) 他們還沒到。

(C) 他們要什麼時候都可以。

track 154

26. (M-Am): Did you reserve a table for the welcome party?

(W-Br):　(A) They haven't done it.

　　　　　(B) It has arrived.

　　　　　(C) I forgot it.

26.（男－美）：你為歡迎餐會預訂好了嗎？

　　（女－英）：(A) 他們還沒。

　　　　　　　(B) 到了。

　　　　　　　(C) 我忘了。

27. (W-Am): How long has Mr. Chang worked for the company?

(M-Br):　(A) Not in the Asian region.

　　　　　(B) For quite a few years.

　　　　　(C) Not far from here.

27.（女－美）：張先生在這家公司工作多久了？

　　（男－英）：(A) 不在亞洲區。

　　　　　　　(B) 好幾年了。

　　　　　　　(C) 離這裡不遠。

28. (M-Cn): Should we hire more people with disabilities or not?

(W-Aus): (A) Let's interview more people to decide it.

　　　　　(B) We don't have the time.

　　　　　(C) We've never been to the office.

28.（男－加）：我們該多雇用幾個身心障礙者嗎？

（女－澳）：(A) 我們再多面試幾個再決定。

(B) 我們沒有時間。

(C) 我們不曾到過那公司。

 track 155

29. (M-Aus): Isn't the new sales assistant good at writing English texts?

(W-Am): (A) The rules should be clearly written.

(B) The texts are written in good English.

(C) Do you need his help with English writing?

29.（男－澳）：這個新來的業務助理不是很擅長寫英文？

（女－美）：(A) 這些規則應該要清楚寫下。

(B) 這些文章是用優美英文寫下的。

(C) 你需要他幫你寫英文嗎？

30. (W-Cn): The application has been processed, hasn't it?

(M-Br): (A) You need to order some more.

(B) The catalog has been sent out.

(C) The result will come out soon.

30.（女－加）：已經在審核申請了吧？

（男－英）：(A) 你必須要訂多一些。

(B) 型錄已經寄出。

(C) 結果很快就會出來。

31. (M-Aus): How come you've never talked in the weekly meeting?

(W-Am): (A) Maybe it will do.

(B) I haven't got any chance.

(C) When is the best time?

31.（男－澳）：為什麼妳在週會都不曾發言？

（女－美）：(A) 或許這樣就可以。

(B) 我沒有任何機會。

(C) 什麼時候最好？

Part
3　簡短對話

Directions: You will hear some conversations between two or more people. You will be asked to answer three questions about what the speakers say in each conversation. Select the best response to each question and mark the letter (A), (B), (C), or (D) on your answer sheet. The conversations will not be printed in your test book and will be spoken only one time.

　　解說：你會聽到兩人或多人之間的對話，你必須要回答關於每段對話的三個問題，請選出每個問題的最佳答案，然後在答案紙上劃記 (A) 或 (B) 或 (C) 或 (D)，這些對話不會在你的測驗本上印出來，而且只會播放一次。

track 156

(1)

(M-Am): Why did you reject my application of travel subsidies for my business trip to Thailand?

(W-Br): You didn't submit sufficient documents for the paperwork.

(M-Am): What is missing?

(W-Br): Receipts of transportation, such as train and taxi fees.

(M-Am): I see.

(W-Br): You will have to submit them within two weeks so that your application will be regarded valid.

（男－美）：為什麼我出差交通補助申請被拒絕了呢？

（女－英）：你沒有繳交文書作業需要的足夠文件。

（男－美）：缺什麼呢？

（女－英）：交通費用收據，像是火車與計程車費用。

（男－美）：了解。

（女－英）：你必須要在兩個星期內繳交，這樣你的申請才能生效。

track 156

32. What is probably the woman's position in the com pany?

(A) CEO.

(B) Public Relationship officer.

(C) Senior accountant.

(D) Media contact person.

32. 這女子在公司的職位可能是什麼？

(A) 執行長。

(B) 公關。

(C) 資深會計。

(D) 媒體聯絡人。

33. What did the woman ask the man to do?

(A) To provide enough documents.

(B) To do all the work.

(C) To make adjustments.

(D) To go to another country.

33. 女子要求男子做什麼？

(A) 提供足夠文件。

(B) 做所有工作。

(C) 做修改。

(D) 到其他國家。

track 157

34. How much time does the woman give the man?

(A) A month.

(B) A fortnight

(C) A year.

(D) A week.

34. 女子給男子多久時間？

(A) 一個月。

(B) 兩星期。

(C) 一年。

(D) 一星期。

(2)

(W-Aus): Welcome to Sydney. Our CEO asked me to take you to the venue, where the conference is going to take place tonight.

(M-Am): Your CEO will host the event, and besides me, there are three other keynote speakers. Am I right?

(W-Aus): Yes, that's correct, and your topic is your specialty, climate change and its effects on world economics.

(M-Am): Can I have time to answer questions from the audience?

(W-Aus): Not really, due to time limit. We'll be lucky if we have time for all guest speakers to have some discussion.

(M-Am): That's fine with me.

track 157

（女－澳）：歡迎來到雪梨，我們執行長要我帶您去今晚的會議場所看一下。

（男－美）：你們的執行長會主持活動，除了我之外，有 3 位主題演講人，是這樣嗎？

（女－澳）：完全正確，您的主題是您的專長，氣候變遷與其對全球經濟的影響。

（男－美）：有時間讓我回答觀眾的問題嗎？

（女－澳）：沒有呢，因為時間有限。如果所有來賓還有時間討論，就算我們很幸運了。

（男－美）：我沒問題。

35. What is the man coming to Sydney for?

(A) To inspect factories.

(B) To visit a company.

(C) To attend a conference.

(D) To travel around.

35. 男子到雪梨的目的為何？

(A) 檢查工廠。

(B) 拜訪公司。

(C) 開會。

(D) 到處旅遊。

36. How many keynote speakers all together are there in the conference?

(A) 5.

(B) 4.

(C) 3.

(D) 2.

36. 這場會議共有幾位主題演講人？

(A) 5 人。

(B) 4 人。

(C) 3 人。

(D) 2 人。

37. Why does the woman say there will be no Q & A sessions?

(A) There are no questions.

(B) They do not have audience.

(C) The CEO does not want it.

(D) There is not sufficient time.

37. 為什麼女子說沒有回答觀眾問題時間？

(A) 沒有問題。

(B) 他們沒有觀眾。

(C) 執行長不想要有。

(D) 沒有足夠時間。

(3)

(M-Am): Look! The Japanese exchange rate is 1 JPY = 0.278 TWD.

(W-Br): Japanese Yen is getting weaker and weaker.

(M-Am): Good news for us travelling to Japan, and bad news for the Japanese coming to Taiwan.

(W-Br): In that case, I'm going to exchange some Taiwanese dollars for Japanese Yen now. Maybe soon there is a chance to travel to Japan.

(M-Am): I am in.

（男－美）：你看！日幣匯率 1：0.278。

（女－英）：日幣越來愈貶值。

（男－美）：對於我們去日本旅行者是好消息，對日本來台者則是壞消息。

（女－英）：這樣的話，現在我要用台幣換些日幣，或許很快就會有去日本旅行的機會。

（男－美）：我也要。

38. Where are the two people probably at?

(A) A church.

(B) A department store.

(C) A hospital.

(D) A bank.

38. 這兩人可能在什麼地方？

(A) 教堂。

(B) 百貨公司。

(C) 醫院。

(D) 銀行。

 track 159

39. How does the Japanese Yen perform?

(A) It reached an all-time high.

(B) Its value against TWD is getting low.

(C) It is very strong now.

(D) It fluctuates very much.

39. 日幣行情如何？

(A) 來到史上最高。

(B) 對台幣匯率越來越低。

(C) 現在非常好。

(D) 變動很大。

40. What does the man mean by saying "I am in."?

(A) I know what you mean.

(B) I agree with you.

(C) I trust you.

(D) Count me in.

40. 男子說" **I am in.** "的意思是？

(A) 我知道妳的意思。

(B) 我同意妳。

(C) 我相信妳。

(D) 我也要。

(4)

(M-Br): Have you come up with some good lottery gift ideas for the End-of-Year Party?

(W-Am): Quite a few.

(M-Br): Let's hear it then.

(W-Am): The first option is the 3C products from our own factory, and the second choice is the wearable digital gadgets, subsidized by Sunshine Company.

(M-Br): I would go for the first one. Although we work on some projects with the teams from Sunshine Company, sometimes we are kind of like competitors with each other.

(W-Am): That makes sense.

（男－英）：妳想到了一些尾牙的抽獎禮物點子了嗎？

（女－美）：還不少呢。

（男－英）：說來聽聽。

（女－美）：第一選項是我們自家工廠的 3C 產品；第二個選項是陽光公司贊助的可穿式數位裝置。

（男－英）：我會選第一選項。雖然我們跟陽光公司在一些專案有合作，有時我們有點像是競爭對手。

（女－美）：有道理。

track 160

41. What is the main subject the two people are talking about?

(A) Bonus.

(B) Performers.

(C) Lottery gifts.

(D) Catering.

41. 兩人的談話主題為何？

(A) 紅利。

(B) 表演者。

(C) 抽獎獎品。

(D) 外燴。

42. Why does the woman prefer not to adopt the second option?

(A) Due to the subsidizing company.

(B) Due to the poor quality of the products.

(C) Due to insufficient gift numbers.

(D) Due to the old-fashioned design.

42. 為什麼女子比較不想要第二個選擇？

(A) 因為贊助廠商。

(B) 因為產品品質差。

(C) 因為禮物數目不夠。

(D) 因為設計老式。

track 160

43. What does man mean by "kind of"?

(A) Especially.

(B) Typically.

(C) Besides.

(D) Somewhat.

43. 男子說 "**kind of**" 是什麼意思？

(A) 特別地。

(B) 常見地。

(C) 除此之外。

(D) 有點。

(5)

(M-Am): Have you seen the Taiwan Travel Subsidy Program in the newspaper?

(W-Br): No, I haven't heard of it.

(M-Am): This year from September 1 to October 31, you get 1000 TWD subsidy.

(W-Br): What's more, with your booking for one night, you can have 200 TWD vouchers for hot spring and 200 TWD vouchers for night market.

(M-Am): That sounds great. Maybe I'll take my family to the eastern coast soon.

(W-Br): That's a good idea. The only criterion for

applying for it is to have a Taiwanese identification card.

(M-Am): I'll ask my husband to book the accommodation now. He has a Taiwanese ID.

（女－美）：妳看到了報紙上刊登的台灣旅遊補助嗎？

（男－英）：我沒有聽說呢。

（女－美）：從今年 9 月 1 日到10月31日為止，如果你預定一個房間，就可以得到1000元補助。

（男－英）：還有，訂一晚房間就可以獲得200元溫泉折價券與200元夜市折價券。

（女－美）：聽來真讚，或許我很快就會帶我家人去東岸旅行。

（男－英）：這主意很好。唯一申請的條件是要有台灣身分證。

（女－美）：我會請我老公現在就去預訂住宿，他有台灣身分證。

 track 161

44. What is the topic of their discussion?

(A) Night market snacks.

(B) A discount for transportation.

(C) A subsidy program for tourism.

(D) Free hot spring visits.

44. 他們討論的主題為何？

(A) 夜市點心。

(B) 交通費用折扣。

(C) 觀光補助。

(D) 免費溫泉旅。

45. How much subsidy can a Taiwanese get for booking one night and a hot spring?

(A) Not mentioned here.

(B) 1000 NTD.

(C) 1200 NTD.

(D) 1400 NTD.

45. 台灣人訂房一晚加上溫泉服務可以得到多少補助？

(A) 這裡沒有提及。

(B) 1000 台幣。

(C) 1200 台幣。

(D) 1400 台幣。

46. What does the woman mean by "the only criteria"?

(A) the only condition.

(B) the extra bonus.

(C) the discounted price.

(D) the best service.

46. 女子說 "**the only criterion**" 的意思為何？

(A) 唯一條件。

(B) 多餘紅利。

(C) 折扣後價格。

(D) 最好的服務。

track 162

(6)

(W-Am): Good morning! Our Farmers Market is open every day from 8:30 a.m. to 2:30 p.m.

(M-Br): What distinguishes your market from others?

(W-Am): The produce sold here is from the region and is organic. One hour before the market closes, we have a special sale and all items are 40% off.

(M-Br): That sounds fantastic.

(W-Am): Right now, it is December and we have a special section of Christmas gifts.

（女－美）：早安！我們的農友市集每天早上 8:30 開，營業至下午2:30。

（男－英）：你們市集跟別的相比有何特殊之處？

（女－美）：我們這裡銷售的農產品都是當地所產，而且是有機的。結束營業 1 個小時前，我們有特賣，所有商品都打 6 折。

（男－英）：聽來很不錯。

（女－美）：現在是12月，我們有聖誕禮物專區。

track 162

47. What is special about this Farmers Market?

(A) They sell organic produce from the area.

(B) They sell handicraft items.

(C) They have bags designed by local artists.

(D) They have hand-made gifts.

47. 這個農友市集有何特殊之處？

(A) 他們賣的有機農產品都是當地所產。

(B) 他們賣手工藝品。

(C) 他們有在賣當地藝術家設計的包包。

(D) 他們有手作的禮物。

48. At what time can the customers receive a special discount at the market?

(A) Nine o'clock in the morning.

(B) One o'clock in the afternoon.

(C) Eight thirty in the morning.

(D) One thirty in the afternoon.

48. 什麼時候顧客可以有市集特別折扣？

(A) 早上 9 點。

(B) 下午 1 點。

(C) 早上 8:30。

(D) 下午 1:30。

49. What does the Farmers Market offer especially in December?

(A) Winter clothes.

track 162

(B) Gingerbread.

(C) Red wine.

(D) Christmas Presents.

49. 農友市集**12**月有提供什麼特別活動？

(A) 冬天衣物。

(B)薑餅。

(C) 紅酒。

(D) 聖誕節禮物。

track 163

(7)

(M-Am): Hello, is it your first visit to this flea market in San Francisco?

(W-Br): That's right. I am here to visit my daughter, who is studying here.

(M-Am): We have preciously rare and nostalgic dolls and handicraft works, pictures and graphics, second-hand books and records, and almost anything you can think of.

(W-Br): I am thinking of buying a souvenir to take home for my neighbor because she waters my plants while I am not at home.

(M-Am): What about the handmade artwork of wood carving? It is on sale now and costs only 10 USD.

(W-Br): That's a bargain. I'll take it.

track 163

（男－美）：哈囉，這是妳第一次來到舊金山的跳蚤市場嗎？

（女－英）：是啊，我來這兒是為了看我女兒，她在這裡讀書。

（男－美）：我們有珍貴稀有的懷舊玩偶、手工藝品、照片與圖片、二手書與唱片，還有幾乎任何妳想得到的東西。

（女－英）：我想要買個紀念品帶回去給我的鄰居，因為我不在家時她會幫我澆花。

（男－美）：這個木雕手工藝品如何？現在正在大拍賣，只要10美金。

（女－英）：真划算，我買了。

50. What can be said about the items sold at the flea market?

(A) Only handmade dolls.

(B) Old second-hand things.

(C) All sorts of items.

(D) Souvenirs from that region.

50. 關於這些於此跳蚤市場所賣的物件，何者為正確？

(A) 只有手工藝玩偶。

(B) 只有二手東西。

(C) 各式各樣的物件。

(D) 那個地區的紀念品。

51. What does the man suggest the woman to buy?

(A) Handicraft wood works.

(B) Homemade sweets.

(C) Designed graphics.

(D) Books and records.

51. 男子建議女子買什麼？

(A) 手工木雕品。

(B) 自製甜點。

(C) 設計圖片。

(D) 書與唱片。

52. Why does the woman mean by saying "That's a bargain"?

(A) The item is rare.

(B) The price is good.

(C) The artwork is handmade.

(D) The product is popular.

52. 女子說 **"That's a bargain"** 是什麼意思？

(A) 這個物件很稀有。

(B) 價錢很好。

(C) 這個藝術品是手作的。

(D) 產品很受歡迎。

track 164

(8)

(M-Am): Hello Ms. Brown, could you tell us something about yourself?

(W-Aus): I majored in Management of Information Technology, and I worked for Microsoft for four years.

(M-Am): What makes you think you are the ideal candidate for this position?

(W-Aus): In the job description, you are looking for a talented person with smart phone App design. This is what I specialize in, and I would like to join your team of Research and Development very much.

(M-Am): When can you start to work?

(W-Aus): I have to give my current employer one-month notice before quitting my job. In the meantime, I'll need to deal with the handover properly.

（男－美）：布朗小姐您好，可不可以請您跟我們稍微介紹妳自己一下？

（女－澳）：我主修資訊科技管理，我曾經為微軟工作了四年。

（男－美）：為什麼您認為您是這個職缺最適合人選？

（女－澳）：在工作內容中，您在找的是具有智慧型手機應用軟體設計天分的人，這正是我的專長，我非常想要加入你們研發團隊。

　　（男－美）：妳何時可以開始工作？

　　（女－澳）：我必須在一個月前向我雇主提出辭呈，在這期間，我得要做好交接。

 track 165

53. What are they probably carrying out right now?

(A) A price negotiation.

(B) A business deal.

(C) A job interview.

(D) A press conference.

53. 他們現在可能正在進行什麼活動？

(A) 討價還價。

(B) 商業交易。

(C) 工作面試。

(D) 記者會。

54. What field of work does the woman apply for?

(A) Map designing.

(B) Smart phone maintenance.

(C) Social media monitoring.

(D) App development.

track 165

54. 女子要申請的是哪個領域的工作？

(A) 設計地圖。

(B) 智慧型手機的維修。

(C) 社群軟體的監控。

(D) 應用軟體的研發。

55. What does the woman have to do before taking the new job?

(A) Developing a new app.

(B) Handling the handover.

(C) Going through another interview.

(D) Doing a personality test.

55. 女子在接此新工作前，還必須做什麼？

(A) 研發一個新的應用軟體。

(B) 處理交接。

(C) 再通過一個面試。

(D) 做人格特質測試。

 track 166

(9)

(M-Br): Do you know any good cleaning services?

(W-Am): There are plenty of them. It all depends on what type of cleaning services you are looking for, such as routine house cleaning, move-out cleaning and so on.

(M-Br): I am looking for an apartment cleaning service.

(W-Am): I have cleaners from "Nancy Cleaning"

come over to my house for three hours on Saturdays every two weeks, and so far I cannot find anything to complain about their service.

(M-Br): What if I cannot have a fixed time for cleaners to come?

(W-Am): They have an app with booking service for someone like you.

（男－英）：妳知道有哪家好的清潔公司？

（女－美）：有很多家，要看你要找的是什麼樣的清潔服務，例如定時居家清潔或搬家清潔等等。

（男－英）：我要找的是公寓清潔服務。

（女－美）：每隔兩星期我會請 " 南西清潔 " 在星期六來我家清潔 3 小時，到目前為止，我找不到任何可以對他們服務抱怨之處。

（男－英）：要是我沒辦法定個固定時間來清潔呢？

（女－美）：他們有應用軟體供像你這樣的人來訂時間。

56. What is the general topic of their conversation?

(A) Setting up a cleaning service.

(B) Moving services.

(C) Choosing a cleaning service.

(D) Cleaning equipment.

56. 他們的會話內容為何？

    (A) 成立清潔公司。

    (B) 搬運公司。

    (C) 選擇清潔公司。

    (D) 清潔設備。

57. How does the woman think of the cleaning service she has?

    (A) She complains about it.

    (B) She is quite pleased.

    (C) She is very disappointed.

    (D) She does not like it.

57. 女子認為她的清潔服務如何？

    (A) 她很埋怨。

    (B) 她相當滿意。

    (C) 她非常失望。

    (D) 她不喜歡。

58. What service has the woman recommend the man to use in the end?

    (A) A monthly package.

    (B) A deep house cleaning.

    (C) A robot for cleaning.

    (D) An app for home cleaning.

58. 最後女子推薦男子使用什麼？

(A) 一個月的服務。

(B) 全屋徹底清潔。

(C) 清潔機器人。

(D) 一個居家清潔的應用軟體。

 track 167

(10)

(W-Aus): Check this out. There is this information about COMPUTEX TAIPEI 2020 in the Internet.

(M-Cn): I heard this is the largest information and technology show in Asia and the second largest in the world.

(W-Aus): When and where is it going to be held?

(M-Cn): June 2, 2020 to June 6, 2020, in TWTC NANGANG Exhibition Hall, Taipei.

(W-Aus): When is the time for registration?

(M-Cn): From 13:00, Sep. 16, 2019 until all openings are full.

(W-Aus): When can we know if we can take part in the trade show?

(M-Cn): It says end of November, 2019.

(W-Aus): Since you had successful experiences before, I'll let you organize and be the leader the project of COMPUTEX TAIPEI 2020. Let me know if there is anything you need for help. We have quite a few talented IT staff for you to pick from.

track 167

（女－澳）：你看，這是網路上 2020 年台北國際電腦展的資料。

（男－加）：我聽說這是亞洲區最大的資訊與科技展，也是世界第二大展。

（女－澳）：什麼時候舉行？在哪裡舉行？

（男－加）：2020 年 6 月 2 日至 2020 年 6 月 6 日，在台北南港展覽館。

（女－澳）：登記日期是什麼時候？

（男－加）：從 2019 年 9 月 16 日 13:00，直到額滿為止。

（女－澳）：我們何時可以知道是否可參展？

（男－加）：這裡寫說是 2019 年 11 月底。

（女－澳）：既然你從前有成功經驗，我會讓你安排並且擔任 2020 年台北國際電腦展專案負責人，如果你需要任何幫助就告訴我，我們有很多資訊科技專員可以供你挑選。

59. What does COMPUTEX TAIPEI mainly showcase?

(A) Office equipment.

(B) IT products.

(C) Urban design.

(D) Stereo equipment.

track 168

59. 台北國際電腦展主要展覽什麼？

(A) 辦公室設備。

(B) 資訊科技。

(C) 都市設計。

(D) 音響設備。

60. When can they possibly know if they can take part in the show?

(A) June 2, 2020

(B) June 6, 2020

(C) Sep. 16, 2019

(D) Nov. 30, 2019

60. 他們可能何時能夠知道能參展？

(A) 2020年 6 月 2 日。

(B) 2020年 6 月 6 日。

(C) 2019年 9 月 16 日。

(D) 2019年 11 月 30 日。

61. Why does the woman think the man can organize the exhibition well?

(A) Because of her prejudice.

(B) Because of his previous performance.

(C) Because of her lack of IT knowledge.

(D) Because of his humility.

61. 為什麼女子認為男子能夠妥善安排這個展覽？

(A) 因為她的偏見。

(B) 因為他之前的表現。

(C) 因為她缺乏資訊科技知識。

(D) 因為他的謙虛。

(11)

(W-Br): It looks like we can afford to park at this parking lot here. See the parking charge table on the wall.

(M-Cn): You are quite right.

(W-Br): How long do you think we are going to park our car here?

(M-Cn): Let me see… We only have to do our weekly grocery shopping nearly. I reckon less than one hour.

(W-Br): That's not enough for me. I'll need at least three hours all together.

(M-Cn): Never mind. I'm free today so take your time shopping.

	1 hour	2 hours	3 hours & more
Motorbike	$5.00	$9.00	$13.00
Car	$8.00	$15.00	$21.00
Truck	$15.00	$24.00	$35.00

（女－英）：看起來我們可以負擔在這個停車場停車，你看牆上的費用表。

（男－加）：妳說的真對。

（女－英）：你想我們會在這裡停車停多久？

（男－加）：讓我想想……我們只需在附近做每週例行採買，我推測不到 1 小時。

（女－英）：對我來說不夠，我至少共需要 3 小時。

（男－加）：沒關係，我今天有空，妳慢慢採購。

	1 小時	2 小時	3小時 & 3小時以上
摩托車	$5.00	$9.00	$13.00
小客車	$8.00	$15.00	$21.00
卡車	$15.00	$24.00	$35.00

 track 169

62. How is the parking charge based on?

(A) Based on the shopping mall the customers go to.

(B) Based on the vehicle's type and on its parking duration.

(C) Based on the shopping voucher and its valid time.

(D) Based on the banks of customers' credit cards.

62. 停車費的計算依據為何？

(A) 依據顧客所去的購物中心。

(B) 依據車型與所停車的時間。

(C) 依據購物折價券與其有效時間。

(D) 依據顧客的信用卡銀行。

63. According to the woman's planning, how much do they have to pay for parking?

(A) $13.00

(B) $15.00

(C) $21.00

(D) $35.00

63. 根據女子的計畫，他們需付多少停車費？

(A) 13.00 美金。

(B) 15.00 美金。

(C) 21.00 美金。

(D) 35.00 美金。

64. What does the man mean by saying〝never mind〞?

(A) The man does not like the woman to stay that long.

(B) The man thinks the woman can take her time.

(C) The woman does not like to be rushed.

(D) The woman and the man can go home separately.

64. 男子說〝**never mind**〞的意思為何？

(A) 男子不喜歡女子停留那麼久。

(B) 男子認為女子可以慢慢來。

(C) 女子不喜歡被催促。

(D) 女子與男子可以分開回家。

(12)

(M-Aus): Next Wednesday morning I have to see a dentist. Can somebody cover for me?

(W1-Br): I have to pick up our clients from the airport and can't fill in for you that morning.

(M-Aus): How about you, Sherry?

(W2-Am): I have my hands full. You know it's near the end of the year.

(M-Aus): Maybe I should talk to our manager.

(W1-Br): That's a good idea. See what he can do for you.

(W2-Am): There must be something he can do about it.

（男－澳）：下星期三早上我得要看牙醫，有誰可以幫我代班嗎？

（女1－英）：我必須要去機場接客戶，所以那早不能幫你代班。

（男－澳）：雪莉，那妳呢？

（女2－美）：我很忙呢，你知道快接近年底了。

（男－澳）：或許我該跟我們經理談談。

（女1－英）：好主意，看看他是否能幫你的忙。

（女2－美）：他一定有辦法幫忙。

track 170

65. What is the main issue they are discussing?

(A) How to source out the work.

(B) How to fill in forms.

(C) How to find a substitute.

(D) How to cover up a problem.

65. 他們談話的主題為何？

(A) 如何外包工作。

(B) 如何填表格。

(C) 如何找人代班。

(D) 如何掩飾一個問題。

66. Why does the second woman say she cannot substitute for the man?

(A) She is very busy.

(B) She needs to see a doctor, too.

(C) Her hands are hurt.

(D) She does not know how to do his work.

66. 為什麼第二個女子說她不能幫男子代班？

(A) 她很忙碌。

(B) 她也需要看醫師。

(C) 她的手受傷了。

(D) 她不知道如何做他的工作。

67. What have they decided to do in the end?

(A) To postpone the work.

track 170

(B) To change a business partner.

(C) To call an agency for help.

(D) To seek help from their manager.

67. 最後他們決定怎麼做？

(A) 拖延工作。

(B) 換商業夥伴。

(C) 打電話給人力仲介求助。

(D) 請他們經理幫忙。

 track 171

(13)

(W-Br): Do you have a suggestion about the discount rate of these gift items for Christmas?

(M1-Cn): How about all 40% off. We have to sell as much as we can.

(W-Br): What do you think, Jeff?

(M2-Aus): I'd suggest 30% off for Christmas shoppers and half of the prices after the holiday season.

(W-Br): That sounds reasonable.

(M1-Cn): Since you both agree to that, I will keep a record of the sales performance of these items.

(M2-Aus): Great. We will take advantage of the Big Data and report to you if necessary.

track 171

（女－英）：你們對於聖誕節禮品折扣有什麼建議？

（男 1－加）：所有禮品都打 6 折如何？我們必須要盡量賣出所有商品。

（女－英）：傑夫，你認為呢？

（男 2－澳）：我建議對聖誕節購物者打 7 折，假期後打 5 折。

（女－英）：聽來很合理。

（男 1－加）：既然你們兩位都同意，我會記錄這些商品的銷售情形。

（男 2－澳）：很好，我們會善用大數據，必要時向妳報告。

68. What is the main topic they are discussing?

(A) How to select gift items.

(B) How to dispose of the unsold items.

(C) How to set a discount rate.

(D) How to find target customers.

68. 他們在討論的主題為何？

(A) 如何選擇禮品。

(B) 如何丟棄賣不出去的商品。

(C) 如何定折扣。

(D) 如何尋找目標顧客。

5 聽力模擬試題

 track 172

69. What discount rate does the second man suggest after the holiday season?

(A) 20% off.

(B) 50% off.

(C) 40% off.

(D) 30% off.

69. 第二名男子建議假期後打幾折？

(A) 打 8 折。

(B) 打 5 折。

(C) 打6折。

(D) 打7折。

70. What does the second man mean by saying "take advantage of"?

(A) Believe in.

(B) Impose on.

(C) Rip off.

(D) Make good use of.

70. 第二名男子說 "**take advantage of**" 是什麼意思？

(A) 相信。

(B) 強迫。

(C) 敲詐。

(D) 善用。

track 172

Part 4 簡短獨白

Directions: You will hear some talks given by a single speaker. You will be asked to answer three questions about what the speaker says in each talk. Select the best response to each question and mark the letter (A), (B), (C), or (D) on your answer sheet. The talks will not be printed in your test book and will be spoken only one time.

解說：你會聽到幾段一個人的獨白，你必須要回答關於每段獨白的三個問題，請選出每個問題的最佳答案，然後在答案紙上劃記 (A) 或 (B) 或 (C) 或 (D)，這些獨白不會在測驗本上印出來，而且只會播放一次。

track 173

(1)（美國口音）

It is my honor to represent our A+ Foundation to receive the Award of Best Social Enterprise of the Year. My great thanks go to the generous anonymous and non-anonymous donators, who have been contributing to our foundationon on a regular basis. What's more, the unsung heroes of the volunteers, who have made our missions

track 173

possible. As you all know, we have been concentrating to contribute to the education in the remote areas of this country, and in recent years, we have started the work of helping homeless people back into the communities. It is our new goal of the next year to promote the welfare of stray dogs and cats.　With this award, hopefully more people will be motivated to join us to make this society a better place for all of us to live in.

　　我很榮幸能代表我們A+基金會來領年度最佳社會企業的獎項，最想感謝的是慷慨的匿名與非匿名的捐款者，他們定期奉獻給我們基金會，還有無名英雄志工們，讓我們的使命成真。如同大家所知，我們一直專注於偏鄉教育，最近幾年開始幫助街友回歸社會，明年我們的新目標是促進流浪貓狗福利，有了這個獎，希望有更多的人會更想加入我們，讓這個社會變成我們更好居住的地方。

71. Where is this talk most likely to be held?

(A) A ground-breaking ceremony.

(B) A fashion runway show.

(C) A speech competition.

(D) An award ceremony.

track 173

71. 這演講最可能在什麼地方？

(A) 開工典禮。

(B) 時尚伸展台。

(C) 演講比賽。

(D) 頒獎典禮。

72. Why does the speaker say that volunteers are unsung heroes?

(A) They do not have a position in a company.

(B) They receive no recognition.

(C) They do not want others to know their names.

(D) They are forced to do their work.

72. 為何演講者説志工是無名英雄？

(A) 他們在公司裡沒有職位。

(B) 他們沒有得到任何肯定。

(C) 他們不想要別人知道他們的名字。

(D) 他們被迫做工作。

73. What does "stray dogs" probably mean here?

(A) Dogs that have no home.

(B) Dogs that are sick.

(C) Dogs that are away.

(D) Dogs that are vaccinated.

73. "**stray dogs**" 在這裡可能的意思為何？

(A) 沒有家的狗。

(B) 生病的狗。

(C)遠方的狗。

(C)打過疫苗的狗。

 track 174

(2) （英國口音）

Good morning, everyone. Here I'd like to introduce our new accountant, Grace. Before joining us, Grace has been in finance and accounting for over two decades, and she has worked for many reputable companies. As you all know, our previous senior accountant retired 2 weeks ago. He promised to answer on the phone all questions related to the new accountant's work. I hope all of you would help Grace to begin to work together with you in the office. Thank you for your attention.

大家早！在這裡我想要介紹我們新來的會計葛萊絲，在加入我們之前，葛萊絲在財務會計領域已經有 20 多年經驗，而且她曾經在多家知名企業工作過，你們都知道，我們前一位資深會計在兩星期前退休，他承諾要用電話回答所有關於新會計的工作，我希望你們都能一起在辦公室幫葛萊絲展開工作。謝謝大家。

74. What is the main topic of the short talk?

(A) Introducing a new project.

(B) Introducing a new task.

(C) Introducing a new software.

(D) Introducing a new employee.

74. 這簡短談話的主題為何？

(A) 介紹新專案。

(B) 介紹新任務。

(C) 介紹新軟體。

(D) 介紹新員工。

75. Why did the previous accountant leave?

(A) Because he was tired of his work.

(B) Because he took retirement.

(C) Because he did a poor job.

(D) Because he made a big mistake.

75. 為何前一任會計離職？

(A) 因為他對工作厭倦。

(B) 因為他退休了。

(C) 因為他工作成效不佳。

(D) 因為他犯了大錯。

76. How could Grace get help from the previous senior employee?

(A) Via e-mail.

(B) Over Skype.

(C) By text messages.

(D) Over the phone.

76. 葛萊絲要如何得到前資深員工的幫忙？

(A) 透過電子郵件。

(B) 透過Skype軟體。

(C) 透過文字訊息。

(D) 透過電話。

(3)（美國口音）

Attention, all passengers, please. Manila's Ninoy Aquino International Airport is going to be closed due to high winds and heavy rain brought by Typhoon Kammuri. No flights will be approaching or departing from the international airport, and we advise all people take the shuttle buses to leave immediately. Typhoon Kammuri killed at least two people in the Philippines, and the international airport is estimated to be forced to shut down for at least a week. We understand that thousands of passengers will be affected by this, including the athletes from abroad for Southeast

track 175

Asian Games. As soon as the reopening date is available, we will announce it on the official website of the airport, along with all new flight details. Please accept our apology and thank you for your cooperation.

各位乘客請注意，馬尼拉尼諾伊亞基諾國際機場將會因為颱風北冕所挾帶的強風豪雨而關閉，所有班機都禁止進出

此國際機場，所有人都請搭接駁車快速離開。颱風北冕造成菲律賓至少兩人死亡，此國際機場估計被迫關閉至少一星期，我們了解無數的乘客會受此影響，包括來參加東亞運的國外運動員。我們會儘快在機場官網上公布機場重新開放日期，還有新班級資料。請接受我們的道歉，並謝謝您配合。

77. What does the announcement mainly about?

(A) The airport is flooded.

(B) The airport is over-crowded.

(C) The airport is going to be shut down.

(D) The airport is going to be repaired.

77. 這個宣告的主題為何？

(A) 機場淹水了。

(B) 機場過度擁擠。

(C) 機場快要關閉了。

(D) 機場快要整修。

 track 176

78. How long is the airport going to be closed for?

(A) It's not going to be closed.

(B) More than 7 days.

(C) Less than 7 days.

(D) Not mentioned here.

78. 機場還要關閉多久?

(A) 沒有要關閉。

(B) 多於 7 天。

(C) 少於 7 天。

(D) 這裡沒有提及。

79. What does the word〝available〞here closest in meaning to?

(A) accessible.

(B) made known.

(C) approaching

(D) made easy

79. 這裡的〝**available**〞意思最接近下列哪一個?

(A) 可接近。

(B) 公開。

(C) 來到。

(D) 變容易。

track 176

(4)（加拿大口音）

Good evening, everyone, this is Jason from the J & J News Radio Station. On HoPing East Rd Sec 3 there is a deadly crash of motorcycle and a taxi. The police and the ambulance workers arrived about five minutes ago and are trying to rescue motorist. The spot where the accident occurred was blocked and no traffic would be allowed through. This caused serious traffic jams to the bumper-to-bumper traffic at the rush hour. To avoid being delayed, drivers are advised to take other alternative routes if possible. Please stay tuned to the J & J News Radio Station at all times to keep informed about the latest development of the accident.

大家晚安，我是 J & J 新聞電台的傑森。在和平東路三段有一場摩托車與計程車相撞的車禍，警察和救護車人員於 5 分鐘前抵達，現在正努力急救機車騎士，車禍現場已經圍堵起來，不准任何人車進入，原本交通巔峰時間車流就擁擠，現在交通堵塞因此更加嚴重。為避免受到拖延，我們建議駕駛者如果可能的話改採取其它路線，請隨時鎖定 J & J 新聞電台，我們會為您隨時更新車禍的最新發展。

track 177

80. What is this report mainly about?

(A) A new motorcycle.

(B) A traffic accident.

(C) A radio station host.

(D) A radio advertisement.

80. 這個報導主題為何？

(A) 一台新摩托車。

(B) 一場交通車禍。

(C) 一位電台主持人。

(D) 一則廣播廣告。

81. When does the accident most likely to happen?

(A) Weekend.

(B) Lunch hour.

(C) Breakfast time.

(D) Commuting time.

81. 這場車禍最容易發生於什麼時候？

(A) 周末。

(B) 午餐時。

(C) 早餐時。

(D) 通勤時。

82. What does the word "alternative" possibly mean here?

(A) Other.

(B) Next.

(C) Native.

(D) Taken.

82. 這裡的 **"alternative"** 這個字可能是什麼意思？

(A) 其它的。

(B) 下一個。

(C) 當地的。

(D) 已有人用的。

(5)（澳洲口音）

Hello everyone, welcome to Pingxi, the only place where Sky Lantern is officially allowed in Taiwan.

Please look up and you will see many colorful sky lanterns in the sky.

Today it is the Lantern Festival, the last day of the Lunar New Year, and the Pingxi Lantern Festival is most spectacular of all events on the festive day.

People write their wishes and prayers on the sky lanterns and launch them together from the Shifen Sky Lantern Square.

I won't talk anymore because I can see you are all eager to try. Let's choose the lanterns and write wishes on them!

track 178

　　大家好，歡迎來到平溪，台灣唯一合法放天燈的地方，請抬頭向上看，您會看見天上有很多彩色的天燈，今天是元宵節，農曆春節的最後一天，平溪天燈節是當日最熱鬧的慶典，人們在天燈上寫下他們的祈願和祝福，然後一起在十分天燈廣場上一起施放，我不再多說了，因為我看你們都迫不及待想試看看。現在我們來挑天燈，寫下祝福吧。

83. **What is the purpose of the tour?**

    (A) To taste special food for the lantern festival.

    (B) To experience the Sky Lantern Festival.

    (C) To take photos of lanterns.

    (D) To launch fireworks from the square.

83. 這旅程的目的為何？

    (A) 體驗元宵美食。

    (B) 體驗天燈節。

    (C) 拍照燈籠。

    (D) 在廣場上放煙火。

84. **What will be written on the Sky Lanterns?**

    (A) Dates of the festival.

    (B) Terrible thoughts.

    (C) Prayers and wishes.

    (D) Dates of birthdays.

track 178

84. 人們在天燈上寫些什麼？

(A) 節慶的日期。

(B)糟糕的想法。

(C) 祈願和祝福。

(D) 生日的日期。

85. Why does the guide say "I won't talk any more"?

(A) Because people are bored.

(B) Because people want to leave.

(C) Because people are not polite.

(D) Because people are ready to try.

85. 為什麼導遊說"我不再多説了"？

(A) 因為大家都感到無聊。

(B) 因為大家都想要離開。

(C) 因為大家沒禮貌。

(D) 因為大家都迫不及待想試看看。

 track 179

(6)（美國口音）

Good morning, this is Sandy Liu from Taiwan Bank. Sorry I wasn't here when you asked for information about life insurance in our bank. Now I have all the suitable insurance options ready for you. Could you please let me know what time suits you best for you to come in. I'd

track 179

like to explain to you in person the details and help you make the right choices. If you need, I can also help you fill out some paperwork. I am available except Wednesday afternoon and Friday morning. Thank you and hope to see you soon.

早安，我是台灣銀行的劉珊蒂，不好意思，您向我們詢問壽險時我不在，現在我準備好了所有適合您的保險方案，請讓我知道什麼時間進公司對您最方便，我想為您親自解釋相關細節，並且幫助您做最佳選擇。如果您有需要，我可以協助您填寫一些文件。除了星期三下午和星期五上午，我都有空，謝謝您，希望能很快再見到您。

86. What is the main subject of the message?

(A) Arranging a good time to discuss issues.

(B) Insuring against fire and flood.

(C) Discussing a business proposal.

(D) Taking a loan to start business.

86. 這個留言的主題為何？

(A) 安排討論事情的合適時間。

(B) 火險與洪水險。

(C) 討論商業提案。

(D) 貸款創業。

87. Why does the speaker want to meet in person?

(A) To choose a suitable place.

(B) To go through the applications.

(C) To discuss options and go through paperwork.

(D) To make an appointment.

87. 為何說話者說要親自見面？

(A) 為了選擇適合地點。

(B) 為了過濾申請文件。

(C) 為了討論選項，填寫文件。

(D) 為了約定時間。

88. Why does the speaker mention Wednesdays and Fridays?

(A) She cannot make it on both days.

(B) She would like to meet on both days.

(C) She has time on both days.

(D) She has no clients on both days.

88. 為什麼說話者提到了星期三和星期五？

(A) 這兩天她都不行。

(B) 這兩天她都想要碰面。

(C) 這兩天她都有空。

(D) 這兩天她都沒有客戶。

track 180

(7)（英國口音）

Welcome to this press conference organized by Teacher's Union. My name is Rose Chen and I am the spokesperson of Teacher's Union. The labor disputes between private teachers and schools have been going on for quite some time mainly because the Ministry of Education does not have the authority to regulate private schools. Our guests here include Mr. DaDe Wang, who is the head of Teacher's Union and he has been very vocal about defending all teachers' work rights. Other guest speakers are Ms. Lily Huang, a private school English teacher for 18 years, Mr. David Liao, a Physics private school Physics teacher for 5 years, and Ms. Jane Li, the principle of the private Lotus High School. Let's hear their opinions about the recent teachers' strike, and after their talks, we will start the Q & A section for the journalists to ask questions.

　　歡迎來到教師工會所主辦的記者會，我名叫陳玫瑰，我是教師工會的發言人，私立學校老師與校方的勞資糾紛已經由來已久，主要是因為教育部沒有規範私立學校的權限。我這裡的來賓包含王大德先生，他是教師工會的會長，對於捍衛所有教師的權利不遺餘力；其他的來賓有黃莉莉，18年經驗的私立英語教師；廖大衛，5 年

經驗的私立物理教師；李真，蓮花私立高中校長。讓我
們聽聽他們關於最近教師罷工的意見，還有他們發言後
的記者問答時間。

89. What is the main subject of the talk?

    (A) The union fees of Teachers' Union.

    (B) Private school teachers' working conditions.

    (C) The true meaning of education.

    (D) The benefits of being members of the union.

89. 這段談話的主題為何？

    (A) 教師工會的會費。

    (B) 私立教師的工作條件。

    (C) 教育的真義。

    (D) 工會會員的福利。

90. What does〝press conference〞possibly mean here?

    (A) It is a meeting of teachers in the Ministry of Education.

    (B) It is a meeting open for journalists from the media.

    (C) It is a meeting of union leaders and its members.

    (D) It is a forum for anyone who wants to join.

90. 在這裡〝**press conference**〞的意思可能為何？

    (A) 是教育部裡的教師會議。

    (B) 是開放給媒體記者的會議。

(C) 是工會會長和會員的會議。

(D) 是任何人想參加的人皆可參加的論壇。

 track 181

91. What is true about the guests invited in the conference?

(A) They are students' representatives.

(B) They are sales people from the publishing industry.

(C) They are all involved in school education.

(D) They are all from the government.

91. 關於受邀至會議的來賓何者為真？

(A) 他們是學生代表。

(B) 他們是出版業的業務。

(C) 他們都與學校教育有關。

(D) 他們都來自政府。

(8)（美國口音）

Our coffee is not just ordinary coffee. It's Fairtrade coffee. Although coffee is very popular, coffee farmers face many challenges. By choosing Fairtrade coffee, you can help stabilize the coffee prices and improve the production of quality beans. Organically grown coffee farmers can receive an additional price incentive to sustain their production without pesticides. When you purchase Fairtrade

track 181

coffee, coffee farmers in developing countries can have better support to build a better quality of life for their families and communities. Small coffee producers can negotiate better terms of trade, such as fair prices and equal pay for women. In this win-win situation, Fairtrade coffee is truly a sustainable shopping choice.

　　我們的咖啡可不是普通咖啡，是公平貿易咖啡。雖然咖啡非常普遍，咖啡農友面臨很多挑戰，藉著選擇公平貿易咖啡，您可以幫助穩定咖啡價格，並改善優質咖啡豆的生產過程，有機咖啡農友可以得到額外價格獎勵，來維持無農藥生產。在您購買公平貿易咖啡的同時，開發中國家的咖啡農友可以獲得較好的支持，為他們家庭和社區建立更有品質的生活，小型咖啡生產者可以協商更好的貿易條件，例如公平價格和支付婦女同樣酬勞。如此雙贏的局勢下，公平貿易咖啡真的是一種可續性的購物選擇。

92. What is the topic of this talk?

(A) Farming in developing countries.

(B) Organic farmers with a decent income.

(C) The benefits of Fairtrade coffee.

(D) Quality organic beans.

92. 這段談話的主題為何？

(A) 開發中國家的農友。

(B) 收入不差的有機農友。

(C) 公平貿易咖啡的好處。

(D) 優質的有機咖啡。

 track 182

93. What does "organically grown coffee" mean here?

(A) Coffee grown in developing countries.

(B) Coffee produced in the nature.

(C) Coffee produced manually.

(D) Coffee grown without pesticide.

93. 這裡的 "**organically grown coffee**" 意思為何？

(A) 在開發中國家栽種的咖啡。

(B) 在大自然中生產的咖啡。

(C) 手工生產的咖啡。

(D) 無農藥栽種的咖啡。

94. What is NOT one of the benefits of Fairtrade coffee mentioned here?

(A) Better conditions of coffee trade.

(B) Financial support for organic coffee farmers.

(C) Improvement of coffee bean production.

(D) End of poor child labor.

94. 以下何者不是公平貿易咖啡在這裡提及的好處？

(A) 咖啡貿易更好的條件。

(B) 有機咖啡農友的財務支持。

track 182

(C) 改善咖啡豆的生產過程。

(D) 終結貧窮童工。

(9)（澳洲口音）

Bushfire smoke has continued to threat greater Sydney region and has caused serious air pollution for quite a while. The poor air condition poses great concerns for many residents. What can people do to minimize the health problems caused by bushfire? According to experts, there are three things people can do to reduce the negative health impact. First, stay inside with the windows and doors shut. Second, do less strenuous exercise outdoors. This applies to healthy people as well. Third, for those with health conditions, such as asthma, coronary diseases or diabetes, make sure you have up-to-date treatment plans.

森林野火持續在大雪梨週邊造成威脅，對空氣造成嚴重汙染已經很久了，很多居民對空氣品質產生很大憂慮，如何能夠減輕森林野火造成的健康問題？根據專家指出，人們對減輕健康負面影響有 3 個對策，第一，待在室內，關上門窗；第二，在戶外少做激烈運動，即便

track 183

是健康人士也如此；第三，有健康狀況者，例如氣喘、
心血管疾病者、糖尿病者，請確定擁有更新療程計畫。

95. What is the main topic of this report?

(A) Smoking in public is not allowed.

(B) How to protect oneself against bushfire smoke.

(C) Fire drills have to be held ahead of time.

(D) People with certain health conditions should not smoke.

95. 這個報導的主題為何？

(A) 在公開場合抽菸是不被允許的。

(B) 如何保護自己，對抗森林野火。

(C) 火災演習需要提前演練。

(D) 有特別健康狀況者不應抽菸。

96. What is NOT one of the health conditions mentioned here to have treatment plans up-to-date?

(A) Heart diseases.

(B) Diabetes.

(C) Arthritis.

(D) Asthma.

track 183

96. 以下何者並非是文中提及需要更新療程的健康狀況？

(A) 心臟疾病。

(B) 糖尿病。

(C) 關節炎。

(D) 氣喘。

97. What is the closest meaning of "up-to-date" here?

(A) Latest.

(B) Designed.

(C) Standard.

(D) Enough.

97. 這裡的 "up-to-date" 意思為何？

(A) 最新的。

(B) 設計的。

(C) 標準的。

(D) 足夠的。

(10)（美國口音）

Attention shoppers, in 10 minutes we'll be closing and we will have our daily special sale in the bakery section. As usual, most popular items, including all sorts of bread, such as toast and rolls, are up to 30% off. For those who like sweets, various muffins and cupcakes are 20% off. If you are interested in something typical Taiwanese, you'll find our collection of pineapple cakes at the discount of 25% off. Please take a look at the discount board, and don't miss this rare opportunity. Thank you very much for shopping here.

	Discount
bread, toast, roll	30% off
muffin, cupcake	20% off
pineapple cake	25% off

大家好，再過 10 分鐘我們將會結束營業，我們即將開始每日烘焙特賣，如同往常，最受歡迎的點心，包含各式的麵包，例如吐司和麵包捲，最高打 7 折，對於喜歡甜點的人我們有各式各樣打 8 折的瑪芬和杯子蛋糕。如果您對典型台式點心感興趣，您會發現我們的鳳梨酥正打7.5折。請看我們的折扣表，千萬不要錯過這個千載難逢的機會。非常感謝您來此購物。

track 184

	折扣
麵包、土司、麵包捲	7 折
瑪芬、杯子蛋糕	8 折
鳳梨酥	75 折

98. What is the topic of the short announcement?

(A) Advertising the baking class.

(B) Advertising bakery items.

(C) Advertising pineapples.

(D) Advertising discounted cups.

98. 這個簡短播音的主題為何？

(A) 廣告烘焙課。

(B) 廣告烘焙點心。

(C) 廣告鳳梨。

(D) 廣告打折的杯子。

99. Which of the following item has the highest discount?

(A) Muffin.

(B) Cupcake.

(C) Toast.

(D) Pineapple cake.

track 184

99. 下列何者打的折扣最高？

(A) 瑪芬。

(B) 杯子蛋糕。

(C) 吐司。

(D) 鳳梨酥。

track 185

100. How much would one have to pay for a cupcake priced 75 dollars?

(A) 50.

(B) 60.

(C) 70.

(D) 75.

100. 售價**75**元杯子蛋糕，打折後要價多少？

(A) 50 元。

(B) 60 元。

(C) 70 元。

(D) 75 元。

正確答案

1	C	11	C	21	A	31	B	41	C	51	A	61	B	71	D	81	D	91	C
2	B	12	C	22	C	32	C	42	A	52	B	62	B	72	B	82	A	92	C
3	C	13	C	23	C	33	A	43	D	53	C	63	C	73	A	83	B	93	D
4	D	14	A	24	C	34	B	44	C	54	D	64	B	74	D	84	C	94	D
5	A	15	B	25	A	35	C	45	C	55	B	65	C	75	B	85	D	95	B
6	B	16	B	26	C	36	B	46	A	56	C	66	A	76	D	86	A	96	C
7	A	17	A	27	B	37	D	47	A	57	B	67	D	77	C	87	C	97	A
8	C	18	C	28	A	38	D	48	D	58	D	68	C	78	B	88	A	98	B
9	B	19	A	29	C	39	B	49	D	59	B	69	B	79	B	89	B	99	C
10	A	20	C	30	C	40	D	50	C	60	D	70	D	80	B	90	B	100	B

● 後記

　　如果你已經讀到此處，代表你已有足夠耐力與持續的專注力，相信答題速度也於練習中提升不少，也能或多或少應用於實際情境。專注力是做好任何事所不可或缺的，而英語專注力只能靠自己不斷訓練。通常英語母語者不會因為一兩個聽者而放慢速度或重覆，因此花心思準備新多益聽力測驗，練習跟上正常英語速度，在考場和職場都大有助益。相信各位讀者從此書獲得的英語學習要訣，已經大幅提升了英語聽力，一定能獲得金色證照或理想成績，更能將卓越的英語能力應用於工作以及生活中。

分門別類規劃
各個主題的架構！

20個最常見的主題商務

張文娟 著

▶▶▶

職場上遇到要用**英語洽商**的時候，
您是否常會感到書到用時方恨少？

本書 \
整理出各種商務英語常見用法，
讓您與國際客戶對答如流，
溝通無礙，順利達成任務。

Workplace
職場 English
Business Communication
Skills Training
英文王
會話 能力 進階手冊

商務英語 ＋ 常見用法 ＋ 附贈 MP3

關於各主題的簡介　各章生動的開場筆者，幫助讀者進入狀況。
脈絡分明的常用表達方式　分門別類整理實用句型，加上必學實戰的提示。
切合主題的情境對話　幫助讀者從自然的機中學習，提昇職化將英語用以快捷能率。
重點字量庫　字彙是由情境對話中擷取的重要常用單字，並且的字音標和字義。
貼心小叮嚀　此心瞭解各主題商務所該注意的事項，特別強調文化差異與溝通技巧。

張文娟 著

商務英語 常見用法 附贈 MP3

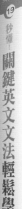

雅典文化

Fast & Easy!
Basic English Grammar

秒懂！
關鍵 英文
文法 輕鬆學

歡迎一起來輕鬆學習英文文法！

■本書的特色：

張文娟 著

特色 **1**
有助高效率學習：
可按順序研讀或當工具書查詢文法，學習效率倍增

特色 **2**
貼近生活：
詳盡解說加上生活化例句，瞬間學會運用文法

特色 **3**
生動圖示：
詳細文法圖示與生動插圖，立刻理解文法規則

特色 **4**
立即驗收：
每章後皆附文法多益題演練，兼具文法考用書用途

特色 **5**
人人都適合：
可作為學生自修或教師當補充教材，適合各類讀者

雅典
文化

讀者可以按照
全書目次的順序來研讀各章，
或當工具書來查詢文法，
也可先做每章後面的
測驗題與多益題，

Fast! Easy
English Grammar

如果發現答題有疑問，
再來細讀此章的文法解釋。

無論是否需要準備考試，

本書所整理的文法內容與生活化例句，

都可以大幅鞏固文法架構，加強文法的運用。

永續圖書
線上購物網

www.foreverbooks.com.tw

◆ 加入會員即享活動及會員折扣。

◆ 每月均有優惠活動，期期不同。

◆ 新加入會員三天內訂購書籍不限本數金額，
即贈送精選書籍一本。（依網站標示為主）

專業圖書發行、書局經銷、圖書出版

永續圖書總代理：

五觀藝術出版社、培育文化、棋茵出版社、大拓文化、讀
品文化、雅典文化、知音人文化、手藝家出版社、璞申文
化、智學堂文化、語言鳥文化

活動期內，永續圖書將保留變更或終止該活動之權利及最終決定權。